THE AWAKENING

BY
JANA DeLEON

First published in Great Britain 2013
by Mills & Boon, an imprint of Harlequin (UK) Limited,
Eton House, 18-24 Paradise Road, Richmond, Surrey TW9 1SR

© Jana DeLeon 2012

ISBN: 978 0 263 90353 9
ebook ISBN: 978 1 472 00709 4

46-0413

Harlequin (UK) policy is to use papers that are natural, renewable and recyclable products and made from wood grown in sustainable forests. The logging and manufacturing processes conform to the legal environmental regulations of the country of origin.

Printed and bound in Spain
by Blackprint CPI, Barcelona

Jana DeLeon grew up among the bayous and small towns of southwest Louisiana. She's never actually found a dead body or seen a ghost, but she's still hoping. Jana started writing in 2001 and focuses on murderous plots set deep in the Louisiana bayous. By day, she writes very boring technical manuals for a software company in Dallas. Visit Jana on her website, www.janadeleon.com.

To my friend, Nancy Lea. You've been chasing monsters for years now, but I'm certain your happily ever after is coming.

Chapter One

Josette Bettencourt stared at the group of workers gathered in front of her ancestral plantation home and for the first time in a long while, couldn't think of a single thing to say.

The crew leader, Ray, a Creole man who was probably in his fifties, stepped forward. "We need the work, Ms. Bettencourt, and the normal dangers of the swamp are things we're comfortable with, but not this."

She took a deep breath and blew it out. "I want you to explain to me again exactly what you saw."

Ray nodded. "We were repairing the fence on the north side of the property when we heard howling, but it weren't no swamp animal that we know. Then we heard something moving in the brush—something big."

"Did you see it?"

"It came through the brush about thirty yards from where we were working. Looked straight at us, then ducked back in the bushes and disappeared."

"What did it look like?"

"It was taller than me by at least a foot or two and had long gray hair. It had a face like a monkey and yellow eyes."

Okay, it didn't sound any better the second time.

"You're sure it wasn't a bear?"

Ray drew himself up straight. "I know bear, ma'am. I feed my family off of this swamp most of the time." He pointed to the crew. "All of them know bear, too. We all saw the same thing."

The men nodded and shuffled around, clearly uneasy.

"I don't know what to say," she said finally. "I will look into it with Emmett, but I'm begging you not to leave."

Ray looked at the men most of whom stared at the ground. "I can't speak for another man," he said, "but I will keep working for now. How many will stay?"

All of the men slowly raised their hands.

Josie felt almost dizzy with relief. "Thank you. Move your crew to the west side tomorrow and work there until I figure this out. Where's Emmett?"

Ray shrugged. "We haven't seen him since he got us started this morning."

She struggled to hold in her frustration. "If you see anything out of the ordinary tomorrow, come straight to me."

Ray nodded and started to walk away, then hesitated.

"Is there something else?" Josie asked.

"You grew up in this swamp, ma'am. You know the legends."

"The legends are stories made up by parents to keep their children from wandering into the swamp," she replied, stubbornly refusing to buy into age-old scare tactics.

"Perhaps, but what I saw today wasn't my imagination and it scared me—a grown man. Stories that last so many years often have truth in them. You can choose not to believe, but please take precautions in the swamp."

Josie softened a little, realizing the man was simply worried about her safety. "Of course. Thank you."

Ray gave her a single nod and motioned the crew away.

She blew out a breath and strode toward the barn, wondering where her foreman had wandered off to this time. Lately, she spent more time looking for Emmett than she did working with him on the repairs needed at the plantation. He'd always been distant and short on words, but since her father's death six months before, he'd moved on to physically absent as well as verbally.

There was no sign of Emmett in the barn, and one look at the sky let her know that daylight was running out. She grabbed a flashlight and a shotgun from a gun rack near the barn door and headed out to the location in the swamp where the crew had been working on fencing.

The area the crew had worked in that day was in the denser part of the swamp surrounding the house. Fences already existed at the perimeter of cleared land, but given the many dangerous creatures living in the swamp surrounding the main estate, the bank was requiring her to maintain a second set of fencing deeper in the swamp in order to open the house as a bed-and-breakfast. The new fencing would also keep hikers from wandering into the more dangerous areas, and provide an extra line of defense for her horses, the only luxury she'd held on to after her father's death.

She pushed through the thick brush on the seldom-used trail until she reached the work area. Cypress trees rose in a thick wall around her and parted at the edge of the brackish water that comprised one of many ponds contained on her property. A stack of posts and barbed wire stood about twenty feet back from the edge of the water, the remains of the previous fence scattered in front of it.

She'd thought animals and the hurricane season had taken down that stretch of fence that her father had installed years ago, but what if she'd been wrong?

The silence of the swamp seemed to echo in her mind. How in the world could something so quiet cause so much unease? She crossed her arms over her chest, unable to remember a time when she'd ever felt at ease in the dense undergrowth. The myths and legends about the swamps of Mystere Parish were as long as the Mississippi River, and although her father had always dismissed them as the ramblings of superstitious swamp people, Josie couldn't help wondering if Ray was right—if those long-survived tales had some basis in truth.

She scanned the work area one last time and blew out a breath, unsure what she expected to find. There was nothing to see here but another afternoon of unfinished work. Another half day of lag to add to the week they were already behind.

As she turned to leave, a twig snapped behind her. She whirled around and looked across the pond where the noise had come from. The sun was setting, creating a dim orange glow over the pond. She peered into the foliage on the opposite bank, but didn't see anything.

You're spooking yourself.

She let out the breath she'd been holding, chastising herself for getting worked up. It was probably just a deer. Then the bushes on the opposite bank parted and a head emerged. It was completely gray and neither human nor animal. Yellow eyes locked on her and she froze. One second, two seconds, three.

And then as quickly as it appeared, it disappeared in the brush without a sound.

The Tainted Keitre.

For a split second she wondered how something so big could move through the dying brush without so much as a whisper of noise, but then common sense took over and she turned and ran down the trail to the plantation as fast as her legs would carry her.

JOSIE CLENCHED HER HANDS down by her sides, afraid that if she lifted them above her waist, she'd punch Bobby Reynard straight in the mouth. The fact that he was currently the sheriff probably wouldn't play to her favor.

"So you're not going to do anything?" she asked, trying to keep her voice calm.

He puffed out his chest, which still didn't force it to extend beyond his belly. "I am an officer of the law. I don't waste my time and taxpayers' money by investigating the ridiculous claims of a bunch of superstitious swamp people, especially when it's all happening on private property. You got a problem at your house—it's your problem, unless there's a crime."

"A brand-new section of my fence was torn down three times in the last two weeks. Vandalism was against the law the last time I checked."

He shoved his hands in his jeans pockets and stared past her out the window, clearly bored with the conversation. "A bear is probably tearing down that fence. Sounds like you're fencing what he considers his territory. Problems with the local wildlife are not problems for the sheriff's department."

She glanced down at his protruding belly and then back at him. "Looks to me like nothing but drinking beer down at the Gator Bar is your business."

His face reddened and he drew himself up straight, trying to suck in the gut and failing miserably. "You better watch your mouth, sweetheart. Everyone may have kissed your butt in high school, but this is the real world now and you aren't any better than anyone else in this town now that all that family money is gone."

"Oh, I imagine I'm still better than some," she said, then whirled around and left the sheriff's office before he could retort.

Not that there was any danger of him coming up with something witty in the next hour or so. Bobby Reynard had been a bully and an oaf in high school and he'd made a profession out of it as an adult. She only hoped some desperate woman didn't marry him so that the cycle could end with him.

"Don't let him get to you, honey, or he wins."

Josie stopped digging for her car keys and looked up to find Adele LaPierre standing in front of her. The spry, little silver-haired woman claimed to be sixty-five, but Josie's mother had always said she was every bit of eighty.

"You're right," Josie said. "But it's just so stupid. High school was ten years ago and he's still stuck there."

"Some things never change. You were the most beautiful girl in high school and you had no interest in him. Now you're the most beautiful girl in the Honey Island Swamp and you're still not interested in him."

Josie smiled and gave Adele a hug. "You always know the right thing to say."

"You're a good girl, Josette. Your parents would be proud of the way you're trying to save their home. Don't let anyone make you feel differently."

She sighed. "All my work is going to be for nothing if I can't stop the vandalism. The crew is already spooked and threatening to quit. Without the crew, I'll never have the house ready to open for New Year's, and without that revenue, the bank will start foreclosure in February. And all that is assuming the work they do isn't destroyed by whoever is doing this."

Adele narrowed her eyes. "Whoever or *whatever?*"

Josie stared at the sidewalk for a moment before lifting her gaze back to Adele. "I haven't told anyone, but I went into the swamp that day and I saw what the men said was out there. I can't afford to tell the truth. People will think I'm crazy. If that story gets back to the bank, they may take away my extension. I shouldn't even have tried convincing Bobby, but I was desperate."

"What if I told you I knew someone who could help? Someone who would believe the real story and find out the truth?"

"I'd say that's great, but I don't have the money to pay trappers and hunters."

"It's a detective agency I have in mind, not hunters."

Josie blew out a breath. "At this point, I'm willing to try anything, but I don't have the money for a detective any more than I do a trapper."

"Don't worry about the money, dear. I've got some savings and I don't think the people I have in mind would try to gouge you."

Josie shook her head. "I can't take your money."

"And why not? My money's as good as the bank's, and if I can't help my oldest friend's daughter, then what in the world do I have left to do with it? We can work out a payment plan later on, after you get the bed-and-breakfast going."

Josie sniffed, touched once again by Adele's huge heart. "I don't know what I'd do without you. You've been such a rock since Mom and Dad passed."

"Your mama was a good woman. One of the best I've ever known. It makes me proud to see her daughter grow up like her. I've got my sons, but if I could have had a daughter, I would have wanted her to be like you."

"Oh, Adele, you completely undo me." She wiped a tear from her eye. "I really appreciate the thought, more than you can ever know, but I can't imagine a detective agency would care about a case that seems nonexistent."

"This one will. An old friend of mine who died years ago had a daughter who just opened a detective agency in Vodoun with her husband. They specialize in things the police won't bother with. I think they'll take your situation seriously."

A tiny sliver of hope ran through Josie for the first time in days. "If you think they can help, then I'd like to try."

Adele nodded. "I'll call the daughter, Alex, as soon as I get home and explain things. She'll want to talk to you, I'm sure, to get more particulars."

"Of course. Have her call me at home."

Adele patted her arm. "Don't you worry, honey. We're going to fix this." She crossed the street and climbed into an ancient Cadillac.

Josie lifted a hand to wave at her as Adele drove off.

What in the world had she just agreed to?

TANNER LEDOUX STOOD ON the dock, staring at his two half brothers, certain they'd lost their minds. "Absolutely not," he said.

"You said you were interested in working for the detective agency," argued Holt, the oldest of the three brothers.

Tanner shook his head. "Not if it means going back into the Honey Island Swamp. I left there when the last day of high school was over and have no intention of returning. Not now. Not ever."

Max, the middle brother, jumped into the fray. "Look, I get it. I wasn't happy about my first case, either, but it turned out fine."

Tanner laughed. "You ended up back in your hometown and acquired a wife. I call that a living nightmare, not fine."

Max shrugged. "Before now I would have, too. Things change and this time it was for the better."

"The bottom line," Holt said, "is that we need you. I'm already committed to another case that's keeping me hopping. I have two cases in the pipeline, but you are the most qualified to handle this one. Max is a good tracker, but he's not you."

Tanner looked over at Max, expecting his brother to launch an argument on that assessment, as he had done since they were kids, but he just nodded.

Well, didn't that just beat all?

Tanner shoved his hands in his jeans pockets, trying to come up with a reason for refusing that sounded even remotely sane. He wasn't about to tell them the truth. The two men standing in front of him had their lives together. The more difficult the task, the more excited they'd be about it. They couldn't possibly understand the baggage he carried around with him that he was unable to release.

Finally, he sighed. "You really think I'm the best person for the job?"

"You're the only man for the job," Holt said. "This case is time-sensitive and we can't afford to lose even a day."

"Fine," Tanner said, "I'll do it."

Holt and Max both broke out in grins.

"That's great," Max said.

Tanner wished he could share his brother's enthusiasm. "So, are you going to tell me what I'm tracking?"

The grins vanished from their faces and Holt glanced at Max, who looked off down the bayou. A bad feeling washed over Tanner. What in the world had he just agreed to?

"It's not a what," Holt said. "It's a who, maybe."

"You don't know what I'm tracking? You said this was a vandalism case. It shouldn't be hard to determine animal from human destruction."

"This case isn't that cut-and-dried."

Tanner felt his frustration with the stalling increasing. "Just spit it out, already."

"The eyewitnesses saw something that matches the description of the Honey Island Swamp Monster."

Tanner stared at his brother. "You *have* lost your mind. I suspected it earlier, but now I know for sure."

Holt held up a hand. "I know how it sounds, but the vandalism is real and the witnesses are credible, especially the one who hired us. Whether it's a man trying to scare her or a real monster, we need to know and we need the vandalism to stop."

"Her? The client is a woman?"

"Josette Bettencourt. She inherited her family's plantation when her dad died and is turning it into a bed-and-breakfast. Do you know her?"

Tanner nodded, afraid the flood of emotion that coursed through him would filter out if he spoke. Yeah, he knew her, all right.

She was one of the main reasons he'd vowed never to return to the Honey Island Swamp.

Chapter Two

Tanner stood at the threshold of the massive front doors of the Bettencourt family home and wondered what the hell he'd let his brothers talk him into. Of all the things in the world he'd never wanted to do, returning to the town of Miel and the Honey Island Swamp was number two on the list. Seeing Josie Bettencourt again was number one.

He lifted his hand to ring the doorbell, then dropped it again and glanced around. No one had seen him drive up. There was still time to leave and tell Holt he'd made a mistake. Max could take the case. He was a decent tracker.

Before he could cement his decision, the front door flew open and Josie Bettencourt jumped back with a startled cry.

Tanner stared, at a complete loss for words. She was even more beautiful than he remembered, and that was saying a lot. Her long auburn hair fell in waves across her shoulders, and the morning sun reflected off her light green eyes. She was taller than he remembered, but still had a body that was both athletic and feminine at the same time.

"I'm sorry," she said. "I didn't hear the doorbell."

"I just got here," he said, angry at himself for fumbling for words. "I hadn't rung it yet."

"Are you from the detective agency?"

"Yes. I'm Tanner LeDoux."

He studied her face to see if the name registered with her. Granted, when he was old enough to make the decision, he'd dropped his father's last name and taken his mother's name like his half brothers, and no one had called him by his first name, William, in years. But he'd wondered if his appearance would create a spark of recognition with her.

She smiled pleasantly and extended her hand. "Josie Bettencourt. It's a pleasure to meet you."

He shook her hand, not sure whether to be relieved she didn't recognize him or disappointed that he'd never left an impression on her to begin with.

"So," she said, "where would you like to start?"

"I read the case file before coming, so I'm aware of everything you told Alex. Has anything happened since you spoke with her?"

She motioned him inside. "I just put on a pot of coffee. Might as well have a cup while I fill you in."

Tanner stepped across the threshold and into the old plantation home for the first time in his life and followed Josie down a long hallway to the back of the house. It worried him that so much had happened in the span of a day that it took having coffee to cover it all. Josie's voice, when she'd invited him back, sounded resigned, frustrated and more than a little worried— none of them good signs.

The enormous kitchen stretched across the back of the house, floor-to-ceiling windows making up most of the back wall. The view of the pool and gardens was beautiful, in spite of the deadness of winter. Pots of poinsettias lined a brick patio and chairs with over-stuffed cushions surrounded an outdoor fireplace. The house had always held a level of class above anything else in town and so had the occupants, a fact Josie's father had been quick to point out to him many years ago.

"How do you like it?"

Josie's voice broke into his thoughts and for a split second, his mind flashed to something other than coffee. One look at her slim, toned body in formfitting jeans and T-shirt was enough to remind him of things he had no right to consider.

"Black is fine," he said.

She handed him a steaming mug of black coffee and smiled. "You're easy."

He took the cup and downed a big gulp of the hot liquid, trying not to think of the connotations of that phrase, either. At the moment, it hovered dangerously close to the truth.

"I like to keep things simple," he said, as much to remind himself as answer her.

She poured herself a cup and added a bit of sugar to it. "I prefer that, as well, but it seems the universe is working against me."

"Why don't you tell me what's happened since you talked to Alex?"

"My work crew found another section of fencing down. They'd just installed it the day before."

"So more of the same things happening?"

"Not exactly. This time it was different." She set her mug on the counter and blew out a breath. "This time there was something red on the fence posts. It looked like blood."

Tanner straightened up. "Did you take a sample?"

She nodded. "I sent it to the Fish and Wildlife Laboratory in New Orleans for testing, but they said it could take weeks with their backlog."

"I'll make some phone calls and see if they can speed things up."

"Thank you," she said, her relief apparent.

"Is that everything?"

"Yes." She looked down, averting her eyes from his.

"Are you sure?"

She raised her eyes back to his. "It's everything that you need to deal with. The rest is my problem."

"Why don't you let me be the judge of that?"

She sighed. "A couple of men on the crew left the job this morning. They're spooked, and I probably won't be able to replace them. Word is out and there are only so many qualified workers around these parts. Most are working reconstruction in New Orleans."

"So you're delayed a bit, but it's not the end of the world."

"If the delays continue, I can't open the bed-and-breakfast on time. I have people booked for New Year's Eve."

"Why would swamp fencing hold up the opening?"

"Apparently, the insurance company considers it a liability if I don't have the fencing and won't write the policy I need to open."

Okay, it was unfortunate, but not a crisis. "You can probably get some workers to come over from New Orleans if you pay a bonus. Worst case, you've have to refund deposits for the bookings and reschedule them if you think the property's not inhabitable by then."

"Yes, I suppose so."

He studied her face, the way her hands shook as she poured the rest of her coffee into the sink. Why all the concern about not opening on time, but the lack of interest in paying a bonus to acquire enough workers to get things finished on time? Surely, not every contractor in Louisiana would be afraid to work in the Honey Island Swamp, especially if the price was right.

She was hiding something, but what? Holt had warned him that the hardest part of the job was figuring out if the things people were hiding were relevant to the case. He hadn't been on the job five minutes and could already see that clear as day. He took a sip of his coffee to avoid sighing. This sort of issue was exactly why he'd chosen a career path in the swamp among the creatures. They didn't present complicated problems like humans.

"Well, if that's all," he said, "I'd like to start by taking a look at the place you saw the creature."

She hesitated for just a moment, and he thought she was going to let out some of what was really bothering her, but finally, she nodded. "Let me grab a long-sleeved shirt and put on my boots. Then I'll take you there myself."

She left the room without as much as a backward glance. He downed the rest of his coffee and stared across the acreage to the tree line where the swamp began. Something was moving below the surface. He could feel it.

The question was, how much did Josie know and how involved in it was she?

JOSIE PULLED ON HER GLOVES as they entered the trail in the swamp. Southern Louisiana rarely got cold enough for the gloves to be a necessity, but the bare branches and dying foliage were sharp and scratched the skin with direct contact. She noticed Tanner had pulled leather gloves from his jeans pocket as soon as they'd neared the tree line. He wore hiking boots and a long-sleeve shirt, which made sense as Alex had told her he was an expert tracker. Even the pistol shoved casually in his waistband only comforted her that she'd made the right decision.

But the rest of the picture was the absolute last thing she'd been expecting when he'd introduced himself as the detective she'd hired. She'd expected someone older, rougher, maybe someone who'd lived in the swamp for a while. Someone with graying hair, scars and maybe even a limp. Or maybe she'd seen too much late-night television.

She shook her head to clear her thoughts. Tanner's looks should be the least of her worries. She had the bank pushing her every day for payment, and hiring a detective was the last chance she had to save her family's plantation from foreclosure. It felt like a long shot, but if it worked, the money would be well spent, even if she had to suffer the discomfort of explaining her precarious financial position. She'd avoided the subject in the kitchen when he'd suggested paying higher wages for workers, but she wouldn't be able to avoid it forever.

She was a bit surprised that Tanner hadn't asked about the creature she saw, but maybe he thought she'd been mistaken. It rankled her that people discounted what she said simply because it sounded implausible, but she wasn't going to lie just to make people comfortable. Now, if only she could convince him to work quickly, her New Year's business might be spared.

"So, Alex tells me you were a game warden," she said, unable to tolerate the silence or her mental wanderings any longer.

"Yeah, I've spent almost ten years in the Atchafalaya Basin."

"But your family is in Vodoun?"

"They are now. Everyone scattered after high school, but my brothers have settled down there now with their wives."

"That's nice."

"I suppose so. If that's what you're into."

His dry tone made her smile just a bit. "It's nice to know I'm not the only person in Louisiana jaded about love."

He didn't respond, but she didn't think much of it. In her experience, most men weren't exactly dying to have long discussions about romantic entanglements. At the moment, the last thing she was interested in was a romantic entanglement, which was a good thing since the tall, muscular man behind her was enough to tempt any woman with clear vision.

Something about his slightly unkempt brown hair and the two-day shadow on his face screamed masculinity in a way she'd never noticed in another man, and during her modeling days, she'd seen many prime specimens. The tanned skin and green eyes only made a beautiful picture perfect.

And familiar.

She frowned as the thought registered completely. There was something familiar about him. It was so brief and fleeting in her mind that she couldn't get a grasp on it, but she had no doubt that she'd seen him somewhere before.

"Did you grow up in the area?" she asked.

"Mostly, but we moved around a lot. Never stayed in any one town for more than a couple of years, except Vodoun."

That probably explained the familiarity. She'd been a cheerleader in high school, and her school had had a big rivalry with Vodoun High School. Tanner looked about the same age as her. She'd probably seen him at a game. He certainly had the build of an athlete.

"Is this the area?" His voice broke into her thoughts as they stepped into the clearing with the damaged fencing.

"Yes," she said, switching her mind back to the present. "I was standing over there, just at the edge of the water. I saw…whatever it was poke its head through the bushes on the far-side bank."

"And it was early evening?"

"The sun was setting, but it was just at the edge of the tree line. The light was still reflected off the pond."

He stepped up to the edge of the water and studied the bank, probably trying to estimate just how good her view had been from that distance and in that amount of light. Apparently satisfied, he nodded and stepped away from the water.

"Did you search the bank on the other side?"

"Not that evening," she said, embarrassed to come right out and admit she'd run for the house like a scared little girl. "But I came back the next morning with the plantation foreman, Emmett Vernon."

"And that's when you took the cast of the footprint?"

"Yes. And sent it to the Wildlife and Fisheries State Lab, along with some of the surrounding soil so that they could estimate weight."

He looked back at her, frowning. "But they couldn't identify it?"

"No. They said it didn't match the print of any known animal in the universe, much less the state of Louisiana."

"But surely, they gave you some information."

She nodded. "They said it was made by a bipedal

creature, over six feet tall and approximately two hundred pounds. The shape was somewhat similar to humans, but with only four toes and webbing between them."

She studied his face as she delivered the description. Everyone from Mystere Parish and likely a lot of people around the country knew exactly what she was describing. All of this was in the information she'd given Alex the day before, but if there was ever going to be a time Tanner called her crazy, this was going to be it.

He gazed back across the pond and jammed his hands in his jeans pockets. "Well, I guess we're going to find out if the legends are real."

Josie stared at him. "So you believe me?"

"I believe you saw what you saw, if that's what you're asking."

"But you don't think it's a swamp monster."

"I don't have to think it's anything. I just have to track it down and stop it from vandalizing your property."

He turned and started off down the bank around the perimeter of the pond. She stared after him, trying to squelch the growing frustration she felt over the entire situation. He was humoring her.

Fine by her.

If he was as good a tracker as he claimed, then he should have no problem finding the vandal. Then everyone who thought she was a frightened drama queen could kiss her skinny butt.

Starting with Tanner LeDoux.

Chapter Three

Josie put her hands on her hips and glared at the plantation foreman, Emmett Vernon. The man had worked for her father since he was a boy—over forty years—but he wasn't going to make it to retirement if he kept up with his current attitude.

"I don't understand your problem, Emmett," she said. "The detective will take a big weight off our shoulders so that we can go back to the jobs we need to be concentrating on."

Emmett took a gulp from his water bottle, swished it around in his mouth and spit it into the hedges near the front entrance of the house. She struggled to keep her cool. He knew she couldn't stand his filthy habits, and she would swear he did it on purpose to aggravate her.

"You mean the business of turning your daddy's life's work into a hotel for snooty people?"

"How many times have I told you I don't have a choice?"

"Yeah, right. You were gone for years prancing on that runway in France. You mean to tell me you didn't get paid?"

"My financial situation is none of your business. You get your paycheck every week. I'm telling you to do your job to earn it."

Emmett narrowed his eyes at her. "You saying I'm slacking?"

She drew herself up straight, not about to back down from him again. "Yes, that's exactly what I'm saying. Half the time, I can't find you when I need you and neither can the work crew. You're supposed to be managing the work on this plantation. Right now that work is in the swamp and that's where I expect you to be, along with the crew."

"You want me to stand around watching people work?"

"No, I want you to pick up a post and help. Like it or not, the days of you standing around spitting are over."

The man glared at her, then spun around and stalked across the lawn to the barn. She let out a sigh and leaned back against one of the huge columns that stretched across the front porch of the house.

"Problems?"

Tanner's voice sounded from the doorway of the house and she jumped. She'd left him inside earlier to have a sandwich and make some phone calls to Wildlife and Fisheries and see if he could get them to move faster on testing the blood she'd found at one of the work sites. She hadn't even heard him open the door. Now she wondered how much of the conversation he'd overheard.

"Nothing outside of the norm, lately," she finally said.

"Is your foreman always so rude to you?"

She frowned. "No, but ever since I went from boss's daughter to boss, his attitude has gone downhill."

"You think he could be the vandal?"

"No! I don't… Oh, wow…."

He sighed. "It hadn't occurred to you yet. I'm sorry I sprang it on you that way."

She shook her head. "You're just doing your job. And no, it hadn't occurred to me, but I don't think it's him. I can see where it would look that way, but I can't bring myself to believe Emmett would betray my father's trust that way, even though he's dead."

"That's okay. You don't have to believe it. I'm going to get proof, but I have to tell you, Emmett's a good place to start. I'll need to know everything you know about the man, and the rest of the crew, for that matter."

"Of course. I have personnel files for all of the crew. I'm afraid that's about the extent of my knowledge of them, but Emmett has been here since before I was born. I can probably tell you anything you need to know about him."

"Except where he disappears to during the day?"

She blew out a breath. "Yeah, except that."

He nodded. "If you'll show me to my room, I'd like to unpack and start on those personnel files tonight."

"Your room?"

"There's no hotel in town and I'd rather be on-site until I figure this out. You're turning it into a B-and-B, right? So I figure you have rooms."

She couldn't think of a single good reason to tell him no—at least not one she could openly state without looking like a fool. But the thought of Tanner sleeping under the same roof sent her body tingling in places it had no right to tingle in.

Unfortunately, his idea made perfect sense.

"Sure. I have two rooms ready on the second floor. One on the north side and one on the south. You can have your choice."

He nodded. "Where is your room located?"

She felt a blush creep up her face. "On the second floor, north side."

"Then I'll take the north-side room."

Her mouth dropped just a bit and she held it there for a couple of seconds, unable to close it or speak. Finally, she said, "You don't think I'm in danger, do you?"

"Until I can figure out who or what is doing this and their motive, I don't want to discount any possibilities. If a man is vandalizing your property, then it's personal, and that's something I want to explore with you tomorrow. If he doesn't get you to take whatever action he thinks he's going to cause, he may escalate. Hiring me may inspire him to escalate more quickly."

A flood of scenarios that she'd never considered washed through her mind. Locked up in her home with the sexiest man she'd seen in forever or alone with a potential madman or mythical creature on the loose.

She wasn't sure which was more frightening.

TANNER ROSE FROM THE small desk that held a stack of personnel files and peered out the bedroom window into the dimly lit courtyard behind the sprawling mansion. On the surface, everything appeared so peaceful, so normal, but he knew something was off balance. He'd felt it in the swamp. Something malevolent was at work below the surface at the plantation.

The personnel files had given him no indication of the problem. The men in the crew were from the area, and Tanner hadn't found anything suspect on them or Emmett Vernon. Tanner had heard Josie talking to someone out front, but he hadn't gone to investigate until he'd heard her voice rise and could make out her accusation that Vernon was slacking. Josie had looked startled when he spoke, and now he wondered what had been said that he missed.

Whatever it was, she wasn't repeating it. Sure, she'd

given him some information, but he hadn't mistaken that flash of fear when she'd realized he was behind her. Whatever had transpired between her and the surly foreman, she didn't want Tanner to know it all.

He sighed. This was so much more complicated than Holt and Max had made it look. In only two months, they'd already solved several cases the police had deemed not viable. At the rate his level of confusion was rising, Tanner seriously doubted he could contribute even a quarter of the success to the agency that his brothers did.

His cell phone rang and he wondered who in the world was calling him this late. Then he saw the number for Wildlife and Fisheries and knew it was his buddy Tommy. Tanner was convinced the man never slept and lived at the office.

"Tommy," he answered. "What do you have for me?"

"Not much, I'm afraid," Tommy replied. "The blood belonged to a rabbit common to the swamp. Without the carcass, there's no way to determine cause of death."

"I understand. I don't suppose you've had a chance to check into the records on that footprint cast Ms. Bettencourt sent in before?"

"Are you kidding me? You call and tell me you were hired to track the Honey Island Swamp Monster and we might have a print cast here—heck, I ran straight to storage and pulled it before I did that test on the blood."

"I was hired to track a vandal," Tanner corrected. "I'm not making any other assumptions."

"Yeah, well, that print was creepy."

"Is that your official opinion?"

"As a zoologist and amateur cryptozoologist, yes, that's my professional opinion."

"Okay, I'll bite. Why was it creepy?"

"Well, everything indicates it's a bipedal creature, but given the soil conditions and depth of the imprint, we're talking something between six and seven feet tall and two hundred fifty pounds or more."

"Bear?"

"With four toes? Dude, don't even go there. Even with a foot caught in a trap, there's no way a bear made this track. Besides, it says in the notes that the next partial imprint was over five feet away. What bear has a stride five feet long?"

Tanner frowned, not wanting to admit outright that his buddy's assessment was correct. "But it could definitely be a man."

"A man with legs long enough to make that stride, yeah. But you're talking about constructing a suit that is good enough for Hollywood filmmaking with all the witnesses that are convinced, not to mention someone agile enough to move through the swamp wearing it. If it's a man, this is the most elaborate hoax I've ever heard of."

"Thanks, man," Tanner said, and tossed his cell phone on the bed.

More dead ends.

He heard the shower turn on in the next room and realized his bedroom must share a wall with Josie's bathroom. Stepping back from the window, he sighed. As if he needed the visual of Josie showering playing in his mind. Josie fully clothed, complete with rubber boots and no makeup, was still far more temptation than he'd ever experienced. Picturing her naked might give him a heart attack.

He'd seen her surprise when he pointed out the advantage of him staying on-site and her discomfort when he'd chosen the room closest to her own, but he wasn't sure what the reason behind it was. She was about to open her house to strangers. Surely, that put her at bigger risk than providing a room to the person she'd hired to protect her investment.

The one thing he was certain of was that it wasn't personal. As a teen, Josie had never even noticed he existed. Her crowd had been the popular kids—the athletes from the "good" local families. Somewhere in town there was probably a loudmouthed ex-jock who called Josie his "woman" and put her in line behind football, hunting and beer. Maybe not in that order.

The scrawny kid doing odd jobs on her family's plantation didn't even catch her eye. Nor did the geeky kid who hid in the back of the classroom. Granted, his mother had moved them to Miel his senior year of high school, so it wasn't as though he'd been around unnoticed for years, but it had often felt that way.

After his father's death, his mother had hopped from town to town as often as she'd changed men. The last one, a trucker with a bad temper and a heavy drinking problem—both of which he'd taken out on Tanner—had brought them to Miel.

And that's where his mother died—holding a bottle of booze and the trucker long gone.

Disgusted that he'd lapsed back into childhood angst and stupidity, he pulled off his boots and lay back across the four-poster bed. He wanted to get an early start tracking in the morning, and it was already close to midnight. If he had any sense left at all, he'd call it a night and turn in.

He stood back up to shed his jeans and shirt, and that's when he heard a noise outside.

Immediately, he flicked off the lamp next to the bed and slipped up next to the window again. The noise had come from outside, but he couldn't tell which direction. The patio lights extended only so far into the massive backyard of the plantation, so his field of view was limited. He was just about to decide it was the normal night sounds of swamp creatures when he saw something moving right where the patio lights faded away.

Whatever it was, it was big. And he knew of nothing that big that belonged directly behind the house at this time of night.

He grabbed his pistol from the nightstand and rushed into the hallway to bang on Josie's door. She opened it a couple of seconds later, with a towel wrapped around her and water dripping from her head.

"What in the world—"

"There's something in the backyard, just outside the light. I'm going to sneak out the front door and around the house. I need you to lock the door behind me. Do you have a gun?"

Her eyes widened. "Yes, of course."

"Get it and hurry up," he said before running down the stairs to the front door.

He heard Josie rushing down the stairs behind him as he slipped out the front door. The hedges across the front lawn provided some cover for him until he was clear of the front porch lights. At the end of the hedges, he slipped quietly across the yard to the barn, which stretched the length of the side of the house, and into the backyard.

It was pitch-black on the backside of the barn. A tiny glow from the moon broke through the dark clouds, but it made only shadows visible and even then, at a distance of ten feet or less, he'd be right on top of whatever was out there before he even knew what it was. Not the best of situations, but it was the one he had.

He inched down the side of the barn, pistol held up near his shoulder, ready to fire, and then drew up short at the sound of dead grass crunching around the side of the barn. Clenching his pistol with both hands, he eased up to the edge of the barn and then spun around the side, gun leveled.

Chapter Four

Josie locked the door behind Tanner and ran upstairs. She grabbed her pistol from the nightstand and checked to make sure it was loaded and ready to fire, then grabbed sweat pants and a shirt and threw them on. She snagged her tennis shoes on the way out of her bedroom, not even bothering with socks.

Socks weren't necessary for shooting a vandal or a swamp monster.

She pulled on her shoes with one hand while unlocking the door with the other. Then, gripping her pistol, she eased out the door and silently drew it closed behind her. Following the same path Tanner had taken earlier, she edged along the hedges and around the side of the barn. Pausing for a moment, she listened to see if she could pinpoint Tanner's position, but no sound reached her.

She took a deep breath and let it out slowly, then crept down the side of the barn. At the end of the barn she paused again and stiffened as she heard the crackle of dead grass around the corner. Her heart pounded in her chest and despite the chilly weather, her hand felt clammy as she gripped the pistol. She said a quick prayer, then spun around the corner, gun leveled.

"Whoa!" Tanner said. "It's me."

She hadn't even realized she'd been holding her breath until it rushed out of her in a giant whoosh. She lowered her pistol and tried to will her racing heart into slowing.

"Did you see him?" she asked.

"No, but I found what was moving out here."

"What is it?"

"Horses. There were two of them wandering around back here. I've put one back in the stall, and was going back for the other one when I heard you and came to investigate."

Panic rushed through her. "My horses!"

She shoved the pistol into her sweatpants, then rushed past Tanner into the open pasture and squinted into the darkness, looking for the remaining horse. Finally, she spotted him about twenty yards away peacefully grazing at the edge of the fence. Softly, she called him and he nickered, then walked over to her, lowering his head to be rubbed. She rubbed his head and then took him by the halter and led him back into the barn.

She flipped the light switch just inside the barn door and flooded the huge structure with fluorescent light. Her heart still racing, she scanned the stalls, doing a mental roll call.

"Are they all there?" Tanner asked.

"Yes, thank goodness."

"I didn't know which stall the other horse belonged in, so I just put her in the first one."

"That's hers," she said as she led the other horse to the empty stall.

Her racing heart was starting to slow and she gave the horse another head rub before exiting the stall. As she slid the dead bolt back into place, she looked over at Tanner, her panic now turning into anger.

"If he was trying to piss me off," she said, "this was the fastest way to do it. The last thing I will tolerate is someone putting my horses in danger, and they did not unfasten dead bolts and let themselves out."

Tanner nodded, his expression grim. "Don't worry. I'm going to catch him."

His voice was so determined that Josie felt her hope rise just a bit. Tanner did not strike her as a man who was good with failure. Maybe with him on her side, she had a chance to get to the bottom of all this.

He stepped close to her and looked directly at her. She looked up at him and forced herself not to take a step back. He was so virile, so male, and being that close to him made her body tingle in ways that had been dormant for a long time. Ways she intended to keep dormant forever.

"You know," he said, "that a swamp monster did not wander into your barn and turn your horses loose."

She blew out a breath, forcing herself to shift her focus from the incredibly attractive man in front of her and back to the night's situation that could have ended badly. "I know."

"You need to think about who has a grudge against you, no matter how slight, and you need to tell me about every single one of them."

She nodded. The last thing she'd wanted to do was lay out her personal problems to a complete stranger, but she was going to have to give Tanner enough information to do his job. "I have an idea where to start."

Tanner looked around the barn. "I don't think he'll come back tonight. Let's try to get some sleep, and we can talk in the morning."

"Okay," Josie said. She reached for the light switch,

but Tanner reached for her hand before she could turn the light off.

"Leave it on," he said, still holding her hand. "He'll be less likely to try something in the light, and if he's foolish enough to come back, it will be easier to catch him."

His hand was warm on hers, firm but gentle. The skin on his hands was rough in some places, as she would expect from someone who worked outdoors, but his rough skin pressed against hers made her instantly wonder how those strong, rugged hands would feel on the rest of her body.

She pulled her hand from his and nodded. "Okay, then. I'll leave it on until he's caught."

Tanner walked out of the barn and she followed behind him and closed the door. They walked silently back to the house, and she couldn't help wondering what he was thinking. Had he felt the same charge she had when he'd touched her hand?

She hoped not, because if he made a move on her, she was afraid she'd abandon her vow to swear off men. And then she'd regret it.

Getting involved with men always led her to regret.

TANNER LOOKED OUTSIDE his bedroom window across the silent lawn. The light from the barn windows created a dim glow around it. When he'd told Josie that he didn't think the vandal would return that night, he hadn't been lying, but there was an uneasiness in the air that he didn't like.

Something was out there…watching, waiting.

Someone thought they were being clever, but to what end was the question. Josie was hiding something from him. He'd known that from the beginning. Maybe after the scare with her horses, she'd be willing to part with whatever she was withholding.

He stepped away from the window and shrugged off his jeans and shirt. What he needed to do was follow his own advice and get some rest. He'd just been thinking about a hot shower when he'd heard the noise earlier, but after seeing Josie all wet and wearing only a towel, a cold shower might be more in order.

Even earlier in the barn, she was still gorgeous. No makeup, wet hair, baggy sweats and she was still the most beautiful woman he'd ever seen. Over the years he'd seen her in magazine ads, usually for clothes, perfume or jewelry. He knew that usually those pictures were altered with filters and software, but for Josie, it wasn't necessary. She was just as perfect now as she'd been when she was a teen.

It had been a mistake to touch her. He could have told her to leave the light on. He didn't have to grab her hand. Certainly, he didn't have to hold it, but he hadn't been able to resist making even the smallest contact.

Her hand had been so warm, despite the outside chill. Her skin was soft and smooth, just as he'd imagined it would be, and his body had stirred from that tiny bit of contact. For a moment, she'd stared at him, then looked confused and just a tad nervous. He'd like to think it was because she was attracted to him, but he knew that was a high school fantasy that his over-active imagination had dug up from the place he'd buried it long ago.

And that's just where it belonged.

He strode into the bathroom and turned the cold water on full blast. Any and all thoughts about Josie Bettencourt that didn't have a direct bearing on the case had to go. He wasn't about to disappoint his brothers by screwing up his first case.

Making a fool of himself wasn't on his list of things to do, either.

JOSIE WAS UP BEFORE DAWN and out the door to check on her horses. Although she'd agreed with Tanner's assessment that the vandal wouldn't return that night, she was still relieved to see everything was in order in the barn. She doled out feed, hay and head rubs to all four of her beauties, then headed back inside to clean up and get ready for the breakfast conversation she'd tossed and turned about all night.

She pulled off her boots in the utility room, put coffee on to brew and hurried upstairs for a quick shower. By the time she came back to the kitchen, Tanner was already standing at the back windows, looking out across the lawn and drinking coffee.

He turned when she came into the room and raised his cup. "I hope you don't mind that I helped myself."

Despite all the stress, Josie found herself smiling. It was hard to be overwrought with worry when there was a sexy man in your kitchen drinking coffee.

"Please help yourself to anything when you want it," she said.

Tanner smiled and she felt a flush run up her chest when she realized the double meaning of that statement. She turned to pour herself a cup of coffee, trying to convince herself that if he took her up on that offer, she'd have the strength to turn him down. She wasn't quite successful.

"You might be here awhile," she said, trying to correct her earlier faux pas. "You should treat my house as if it's yours. I keep the kitchen stocked well with eggs, sandwich stuff and makings for salad. It's not the Ritz, but I don't usually have much time for meals."

"I'm not much of a five-course meal guy myself. I eat most of my meals in front of the television or standing over the sink."

She smiled. "You can use a chair and table here, if you'd like, or the television in the den. I hate to admit, there's television trays next to the couch. Sometimes that's the only time I can catch up on the news."

"A kindred spirit." He crossed the room to the refrigerator and pulled out a package of bagels and cream cheese. "Bagel?"

"I can make some eggs—"

He waved one hand. "Is that what you'd do normally? Or would you toss one of these in the toaster and rush out to take care of your work?"

"You got me. Toss one in the toaster for me. I'll wash up and rinse off some fruit."

She pulled some strawberries out of the refrigerator and rinsed them in the sink, then carried the bowls of fruit to the breakfast table as Tanner placed the toasted bagels and cream cheese in front of two chairs across from each other, with a side view of the lawn.

"Go ahead and take a seat," he said, and grabbed the coffeepot to refill both their cups.

She slid into her chair, trying to get a grip on her nerves. All night, she'd dreaded this conversation. A million times she'd run through it in her mind but still hadn't come up with a way to say it without sounding egotistical and airheaded.

Tanner took a seat across from her and reached for the cream cheese. "How come you don't have a dog?"

Josie blinked. That wasn't the question she'd been expecting.

"Oh, well, we had a hound dog forever, but he passed away a couple of years ago. I thought about getting another when I came home, but I haven't had the time to devote to a puppy. Why do you ask?"

"No reason in particular. I was just thinking that a dog might be good for security."

She nodded. "I guess that's something to think about."

"So," he said, "last night you said you had an idea about who might be doing this?"

She took a sip of coffee to wash down the bagel that seemed to be lodged in her throat. "I thought so at the time, but I think I was just stressed over the situation. Now my thoughts just sound stupid."

"Why don't you let me be the judge of that?"

He looked expectantly at her and she took another sip of coffee. "I've lived here my entire life," she said. "In high school, I was one of those popular girls, but I had big plans that included getting far away from the town of Miel and the Honey Island Swamp."

"Why?"

She blinked. "I...I don't know. I mean, I haven't thought about it in so long. I remember thinking this place was so small and slow that I felt like I was slowly smothering, and I desperately wanted the fast pace and glamour of big cities and other countries. It all sounded so fabulous."

"But it wasn't?"

She frowned. "No. I mean, parts of it were. There are some simply breathtaking places in this world, and I feel fortunate that I got to see so many of them."

"But?"

"But it was hard. I was a model and that business is rather cutthroat. You can't spend much time enjoying everything around you. You're too busy looking over your shoulder for the next person trying to stab you in the back. It just wasn't for me. Then my dad got sick, and it seemed like the perfect reason to come home."

"But there was no reason to stay after he passed. There're other jobs besides modeling. You could have sold all this and started over."

She nodded. "I could have, and I thought about it. I thought about it a lot. But when I returned, it felt different. It didn't feel small any more. It felt comfortable. I knew my real passion was horses, not modeling, and I couldn't ask for a better setup to breed and train. I just need to establish another form of income to support myself while I work on that."

"Makes sense. With the weather here, you can train outside year-round and have plenty of room to grow your own hay. It is a beautiful piece of property, and it only took a glimpse of your horses to see you've got some fine stock...."

"But?"

"But apparently, you think your choice to maintain your roots in Miel didn't make everyone happy."

She blew out a breath. "No. Like I said before, I was part of the popular crowd in high school, but since I'd always planned to leave, I didn't bother establishing close relationships with people. I just hung out with large groups, but it was all very shallow, really. Some boys called me a snob because I wouldn't date them seriously, but it wasn't personal. I didn't have any close girlfriends, either. I just wanted it to be easy when I left, you know?"

"So some people think you're a spoiled snob."

"I didn't say 'spoiled.'"

"The spoiled is implied given the family money

and the fact that your dad probably doted on his only daughter."

"You're probably right. I've already heard the snide remarks about my dad's bragging over my modeling jobs." She sighed. "Which explains the less-than-stellar welcome, but how does that lead to vandalism? It's a serious leap from high school pettiness or even adult annoyance to illegally damaging someone's property. Which is why the more I thought about it, the more I figured it was a stupid idea all the way around."

"Not just illegal damage. This is criminal damage."

She shook her head. "I'd never manage criminal charges. Civil is about all I can hope for."

"Not necessarily. A good prosecutor could make the argument that tearing down the fences might endanger the people living within the boundaries of the fences."

"Maybe, but I'd have to get someone arrested before that could happen, and given my relationship with the sheriff, that's not possible."

"The report Alex typed up says you told him about the vandalism and he blew it off. What's his problem?"

"Me, among many other things. He asked me out once in high school and has hated me ever since I turned him down. He spent our entire senior year playing juvenile practical jokes on me. I'd thought after all these years that he'd have let it go, but apparently, he's determined to hang on to that teenage angst."

"Okay, anyone else you think is holding a grudge?"

"Mack Prevett is buddies with the sheriff. He owns the local bar. I've heard he and my dad quarreled over property lines, and Mack had to move construction of his fishing cabin further down the bayou. I asked Emmett about it, but he said it was old news. But my friend

Adele told me Mack had already started construction and was mad as a hornet to have to start over."

Tanner nodded. "So he has a couple of reasons to hold a grudge."

"He was downright blatant with his dislike for me the one time I dared go in there with Emmett for a beer, but then, he wasn't overly nice to Emmett, either. Emmett just ignored him, of course, as only Emmett can manage."

"Having a beer with Emmett, huh? Given your conversation yesterday, I'm having trouble picturing you two socializing."

"We were picking up supplies in town. Emmett left and went across the street to the bar. I went in after him, but didn't want to make a scene ordering him out. The man is old enough to be my father. So I passed it off as needing a break, hoping he'd take the opportunity away from the house to tell me what's up with him lately."

"I take it he didn't?"

"No. He barely spoke, which is typical. It wasn't a problem when he wasn't being so secretive and obstinate, but now...I don't know what to think."

"Don't worry," Tanner said. "I'm going to look into all options. That's my job."

She sat back in her chair, feeling some of the tension in her neck releasing. That hadn't been near as mortifying as she'd thought it would be. He hadn't smirked or done anything else to indicate he thought she had an overly inflated ego.

"So, what do we do today?" she asked.

"First, I'm going to contact my brother and have him start running some background checks on the people you've mentioned."

"Did you look at the personnel files last night?"

"Yeah, and Max already did a quick check on everyone. All the workers are clean, including Emmett—with the law, anyway. I also talked to my buddy at Wildlife and Fisheries."

Josie stiffened a bit. "Did he find out anything?"

"The blood on the post was rabbit. And my buddy's take on the print is the same as what they told you before—bipedal, over six feet tall and roughly two hundred fifty pounds."

"So we still have nothing."

Tanner smiled. "If it was going to be that easy, you could have figured it all out without my help. We'll dig deeper until we find something. All this means is that someone is being careful, and that takes planning."

"Or the creature is real."

He raised one eyebrow. "I suppose anything is possible."

"So, what now?"

"I'm going to head out into the swamp and see if I can track down your monster."

"Okay. What do you want me to do?"

"Whatever you would normally be doing if none of this were going on."

A wave of disappointment washed over her and she struggled to keep it from showing in her expression. After all, she could hardly expect Tanner to take her with him to track the creature. He was a professional. She'd only slow him down or get in the way or both.

"If you can," he said, "I'd prefer it if you stayed close to the house."

"You don't think he'd try something during the day, do you?"

"I don't think it's likely for anything to happen during the day and right here in clear view of others that may be working around the property, but I don't want you going into the swamp alone."

"Not even to check on my men?"

"Vernon can check on your men. That's his job."

"And if he doesn't do it?"

"I'm going to have a talk with him before I head out tracking. I think we can work something out."

He took a bite of the bagel and stared out the window across the lawn. Josie bit her lower lip and hoped Tanner had some magic words to say to her foreman, because she was all out.

Chapter Five

Tanner was momentarily surprised when his brother Holt answered the phone on the first ring.

"I thought you were busy," Tanner said. "Instead, you're sitting on top of the phone."

"Ha. I happen to be waiting on a call from the morgue. Not exactly my favorite way to start a Tuesday morning and certainly not the way I'd prefer to solve my current case, but that is unfortunately the business we're in."

"Sorry. I didn't mean to make a tense situation worse."

"You didn't. It's part of the job. You learn how to deal with it. The waiting's sometimes the worst part. What's up with you? You ready for me to send *National Geographic* your way?"

"As I did not discover a new species overnight, I'd hold off on contacting the media just yet."

Holt chuckled. "All right. I'll give you at least two days. So, what's up?"

Tanner filled Holt in on the situation with the horses the night before.

"That's not good," Holt said. "I don't like that this has escalated so close to the house."

"Me, either."

"How did Josie take it?"

"Once she was certain all the horses were fine, she calmed down a lot. She's got some backbone. Came out after me, gun loaded. I don't think she would have hesitated to fire it, either."

"It's good to know she doesn't panic. We don't want the clients in the middle of hard-core action, but it sometimes ends up that way. Better for you if the client is someone you can rely on to back you up. Is there anything I can do to help from my end?"

"I need Max to run some names for me." Tanner read him off the list of names he'd compiled based on his conversation with Josie.

"Anything in particular to look for?"

"No. I'm just trying to get a feel for who's here and what their motives might be beyond the norm. Animals are a lot easier to figure out than humans."

"Got that right."

Tanner hesitated for a moment, not sure he should say what was on his mind, but he took a breath and forced it out. "She's lying. Josie, I mean."

"About what?"

"I don't know yet, but I can tell she's hiding something from me."

"Do you think it's relevant to the investigation?"

"I don't think *she* thinks it's relevant, but that doesn't mean it isn't."

Holt sighed. "I wish I had some magic words that would make people air their dirty laundry, but I don't. I deal with the same thing on every case. Some are worse than others."

"Does what they're withholding always affect the case?"

"Hard to say. Sometimes the information could have

led us down the right avenue of investigation. Sometimes it could have prevented us from going down the wrong one. But sometimes, what they're hiding is simply some embarrassing family secret."

"Maybe Josie is hiding something about her father."

"Maybe. She wouldn't be the first person to feel embarrassed or guilty over things her parents have done."

"Isn't that the truth?" Tanner mumbled. He'd spent most of his life trying to hide the fact that he was Walt Conroy and Margaret LeDoux's son, which is why he'd changed his last name as soon as he'd been legally able, just like his brothers had done. That bit of information carried way too much baggage for any one man to find tolerable.

Holt was silent for a couple of seconds, and Tanner knew his half brother got the meaning of his disgruntled statement.

"Sometime soon," Holt said, "Max and I need to talk to you."

"You just talked to me the other day. Now I've changed professions, I'm tracking a mythical swamp creature and living with a lying woman. The way the first conversation turned out, I'm not so sure I want another one with you and Max."

Holt chuckled. "I can't exactly argue with you. But still, when you feel up to tackling some old issues, there's something Max and I need your help on. I'll start these background checks this morning and give you a call as soon as I have some information."

"I'm going tracking as soon as I get off the phone, so leave a message if you don't get me," Tanner said, unable to keep from wondering what else his brothers had in store for him.

"No problem. It might be afternoon before I finish

enough of them to warrant taking up your time with a call."

"I won't be back until I find something or the light runs out."

"Be careful, Tanner. Whatever reason someone has it in for Josie, they're not going to appreciate your butting in. Watch your back, especially in the swamp."

"I will." He disconnected the call and looked out his bedroom window across the lawn. Josie was leading a stallion out of the barn to work him. The stallion's sleek black coat seemed to shine over his rippled body. Tanner knew enough about horses to know he was looking at a prime Arabian specimen worth some serious money.

Josie started working him on the lead and Tanner paused a minute more, thinking what an incredible sight the two of them made. Finally, he tore himself away from the window, grabbed his backpack and headed outside.

He'd seen Emmett Vernon head to the swamp on the south side of the property when they'd been eating breakfast. First thing, he was going to track the man down at the work site and ask him some questions. Then he was going to spend the rest of the day attempting to prove that the Honey Island Swamp Monster was nothing more than a myth used to sell swamp tours and hotel rooms.

THE VANDAL WATCHED THE woman and the horse from the dense undergrowth of the swamp. She didn't appear troubled, much less scared. The work crew had reported what they'd seen, but apparently, Josette Bettencourt was as stubborn as her father.

The man who'd raced outside last night exited the house and started across the lawn toward the swamp.

The man was a problem. The vandal didn't know who he was or what he was doing there, but it couldn't be good. If the man didn't leave soon, he'd have to be dealt with.

No one was going to get in the way of the master plan.

JOSIE HAD JUST STEPPED inside the back of the house for a break when the phone started ringing. Instantly, her lower back tightened and her chest hurt. The first payment wasn't due to the bank for another three weeks, but what if they'd heard about her problems? What if they called the note and ignored the earlier agreement?

She picked up the phone and barely managed to get out a "hello."

"Josie," the loud male voice boomed over the phone, "this is Samuel."

Josie blew out a breath and rolled her eyes. Sam Walker was the local Realtor and busybody. He'd been able to talk people into a coma as early as elementary school. "Hi, Sam. How are you?"

"I'm doing great. Hope you're doing the same."

"Everything's just fine. What can I do for you?"

"Nothing in particular. I was just wondering if you'd given any thought to that talk we had a couple of weeks ago."

"There wasn't anything to think about," she said, trying to control the sharpness in her tone. "I'm not interested in selling."

"No need to get upset over it. I figured as much, but I told the client I'd follow up, so I am. I'll find him something else to suit. I always do."

"I'm sure that's the case." People probably bought

something just to get away from him. "Well, if that's all, I'm kinda busy."

"Actually, I was wondering if you'd be interested in having dinner. I'm free every night this week."

Shocking.

"While I appreciate the offer, I'm not really interested in dating. I've got too much on my plate right now for romantic entanglements."

He laughed. "Not all entanglements between a man and woman have to be the romantic kind."

Okay. Ick.

"I'm not interested in *any* entanglements right now."

Or ever with you.

"Well, the offer for dinner is still open. No entanglements required. You have to eat."

"And I plan to. Usually in my own kitchen and in between tasks. I appreciate the invitation, but my schedule is just too busy right now to take that kind of time off."

"I heard you had a little trouble out there. I figured you'd put off the opening until you could deal with it."

Josie felt a flush of anger run through her. She knew exactly where Sam had heard about her trouble—Sheriff Reynard. That loudmouth wouldn't do anything to help, but he had plenty of energy to gossip all over town about her private business.

"You figured wrong," she said, keeping her voice calm and even. "The bed-and-breakfast will open in time for the New Year's guests."

"Then I best let you get back to it. If you change your mind about selling or the dinner, let me know."

She hung up the phone without forming a reply, not sure she had a polite one left in her. If Sheriff Reynard was telling everyone that she'd come to see him, worried about the delays in construction that the vandalism was causing, they might start to speculate about just how little money she had left. Right now everything was only rumor, but more than a few eyebrows had gone up in town when she sent some of her mother's expensive paintings to New Orleans for auction. People probably wouldn't have to dig very deep to find out just how hard up she was.

If that information got back around to Tanner, she'd be mortified, although she had no idea why. In theory, it seemed stupid to care what a stranger, a hired one at that, cared about her. But for some reason, the idea of him knowing she was broke and making deals with the bank to keep her family home wasn't something she wanted to think about.

Enough people had already guessed the truth. She was going to do the best she could to change her situation before everyone had proof.

Tanner strode down the path in the swamp to where the crew was working on the fencing. With all the construction noise, it wasn't hard to find them, despite the many branches and forks of the swamp trails.

The men froze as he came through the brush, and Tanner could tell they were ready to flee if necessary. "Sorry," he said. "I didn't mean to startle you."

An older man, probably mid-fifties, stepped toward him. "You didn't. You have to be aware working in the swamp, and with the trouble lately, we're paying extra attention."

"Sounds like a good plan," Tanner said. He extended his hand to the man, who he guessed was the crew leader. "I'm Tanner LeDoux."

"Ray Melancon. I run this crew. Are you a new foreman, Mr. LeDoux?"

"Please call me Tanner, and no, that job is still Emmett Vernon's. I was hoping to talk to him. Is he around?"

Ray looked mildly disgusted. "He shows up for a minute or two. Then he's gone. All day, I worry and wait on equipment and guidance, but he's nowhere to be found. This morning was no different."

Tanner frowned. "I just came from the house, and I didn't see him anywhere around the grounds."

"He walked that way," he said, and pointed deeper into the swamp. "About an hour ago."

Tanner scanned the foliage where Ray was pointing. What could he possibly want out there?

"If you're not a new foreman," Ray said, "can I ask what you're here for?"

Tanner smiled. "I'm here to track down a monster."

Ray's eyes widened and he took a step back from Tanner. "You shouldn't joke about such things. The creatures that haunt these swamps don't like to be the butt of jokes."

"Then it's a good thing I wasn't joking. I'm a professional tracker. Ms. Bettencourt hired me to see that the vandalism stops. That means catching the vandal."

"You can't catch the Tainted Keitre. No one can."

"You're probably right, as it doesn't exist, but I can catch a man trying to make you believe he's a monster."

Ray shook his head. "You young people don't understand the swamp like the elders. My great-grandfather taught me everything about this swamp, including the legends."

"And what legend covers vandalism?"

"It's an awakening." Ray looked back at the crew, who'd stopped working to listen. Some of the men nodded. Most just looked at him with fearful expressions.

"You think the creature was awakened? By what?"

"Maybe the construction. He seems to target the repairs," Ray said, but his voice lacked conviction.

"But that's not what you think."

Ray shook his head. "I think the creature appeared because a greater evil is present in the swamp. Something that wasn't here before. It's out of balance. Can't you feel it?"

Because Tanner had always felt the Honey Island Swamp was out of balance, he wasn't sure how to reply. Of all the places he'd lived, the swamps in Mystere Parish had been the only place that he'd never relaxed. All those years in the Atchafalaya Basin and he'd never felt the unease that settled over him after only five minutes of standing in the Honey Island Swamp.

"You *do* feel it," Ray said. "I see it in your eyes."

"Look, the truth is, the swamps in Mystere Parish have always felt uncomfortable, especially the Honey Island Swamp."

"Ah, then you are a man in touch with the ebb and flow of nature. Even on its best day, this swamp is different than others—I'll give you that—but lately, I feel something darker than usual. Something malevolent."

Ray shook his head. "I think it's a good thing that you want to help Ms. Bettencourt. She's a lady and there's not a lot of women these days that I'd call as such, but I know what I saw and it weren't no man."

"Not even a man wearing a hairy suit?"

"A man in a hairy suit can't disappear in the brush without even a whisper of sound. A man in a hairy suit can't make an unholy howl like the one we heard." He waved his hand at his crew. "We know the truth. We saw it. You can choose not to believe, but you should at least prepare as if you do."

Because he couldn't argue with the man's logic, Tanner nodded. "I'll let you get back to it. Thank you for your time."

Ray gave him a single nod. "Be aware, Mr. LeDoux. Very aware."

Tanner stepped past the crew and into the swamp in the direction Ray had indicated Vernon had gone. It was a simple matter to pick up Vernon's trail. The ground was so damp with morning dew that partial footprints showed often in open patches of dirt. The brittle, dead branches snapped easily when pushed or stepped upon and marked the man's passage, as well.

Tanner wondered why Vernon had gone off into the swamp at this location, where there was no clearly defined path. He could tell he'd been moving steadily southeast, but had yet to locate a trail that had been traveled with any regularity. Wherever Vernon was going, he hadn't gone there this way before.

Yet another mystery, when he hadn't made any strides on the first.

He continued through the swamp at a decent clip, his mind rolling back through his conversation with Ray. The man was Creole, and according to the personnel files, had lived in the Honey Island Swamp his entire life. He was not unlike the men who'd taught Tanner everything he knew about tracking, hunting and survival. They were tough men, cunning in their environment.

But Ray was afraid.

That bothered Tanner more than he wanted to admit. He understood the superstitions of the swamp people and those that still believed in the old ways of voodoo and the like. People who believed in such things were naturally cautious and extremely observant, but rarely scared. It quite simply wasn't the way they were made.

He was still trying to make sense of it all when he followed Vernon's tracks around a huge cypress tree and then stopped short. The smell that wafted past him wasn't one he recognized. It was musky, like a skunk, but fouler, like decaying remains.

The swamp, which had been filled with the sounds of insects and birds just seconds before, had gone silent. Not even a breath of air passed over him, and the silence echoed in his head.

He sniffed the air, turning his head to try and determine the direction of the smell, but he couldn't be certain.

Suddenly, a twig snapped, the tiny sound echoing like a sonic boom in the silent swamp. Instantly, he locked in on the direction of the sound, pulled out his pistol and crept toward a thick grove of brush about twenty yards in front of him. When he was about ten yards away, a low growl came from the brush. He paused for a second, trying to place the sound, but his mind couldn't lock in on a match.

He took a breath and lunged forward, hoping to catch whatever lurked there, but as soon as he moved, whatever it was burst from the brush and ran away from him. Over the top of the pile of brush, he could barely make out a mass of gray hair crashing through the swamp.

By the time he ran around the thick hedge of brush, the creature was long gone, but his tracks remained. A huge foot with four toes. Tanner didn't even stop to register the implications before he took off following the tracks through the swamp. He moved as fast as possible, but had to slow a bit when the tracks led into an area thick with decaying vines.

The tracks disappeared in the vines and he stopped to listen. He could hear the tide of a bayou nearby and then a giant splash. He took off through the brush in the direction of the splash and slid to a stop at the edge of a ten-foot drop into the bayou. He looked downstream in time to see a hairy head duck underwater.

He ran down the bank as quickly as the thick undergrowth allowed, scanning the bayou for any sight of the creature. The bayou twisted ninety degrees to the right and he pushed around the corner and scanned the water, but nothing was there.

At least three feet of cypress roots made up both sides of the bank. The creature could have climbed up anywhere down the quarter-mile stretch in front of him, or could have grabbed some air and continued swimming with the tide. He'd scan the bank on both sides, but he already knew it was a long shot that he'd find anything.

He didn't even stop to dwell on the more troubling aspects of the entire situation. There was plenty of time for that later—after he'd had a hot shower and a stiff drink and had figured out what he was going to tell Josie.

Chapter Six

Holt Chamberlain hung up the phone and looked up at his brother Max, who paced in front of his desk.

"Well?" Max asked.

"We got an ID," Holt said, his surprise apparent in his voice.

"A real one?"

"Yeah, a dead, no-longer-breathing but very real and documented person. At least, documented for the last decade."

"And you're sure the tattoo was a match?"

Holt nodded. "I went to the morgue in Baton Rouge to identify it myself."

Max stopped pacing and slid into a chair in front of the desk. "So?"

"Harrison Belafonte. Forty-two. Owned an insurance company in Baton Rouge where the FBI was about to launch an investigation into the possibility that he was using his agency to launder money. Sound familiar?"

"Like Martin Rommel was doing with the restaurant."

"Yep, and I don't think for a moment that it's a co-incidence."

"Did Belafonte kill himself?"

"According to the coroner, he had enough cocaine

in his system to kill an elephant, but he couldn't say whether the overdose was intentional or accidental."

Max blew out a breath. "So is it some sort of organized crime that these guys are involved in?"

"It looks that way, but we have to figure out the connection between Rommel and this Belafonte in order to have any idea where to look for live members."

Holt's phone rang again and he looked at the display, then frowned. "It's the Baton Rouge police."

He answered the phone and listened in silence to what the cop said. When the man was finished, he thanked him and slowly put the phone back in place.

Max leaned forward in his chair. "What is it?"

"We might have our connection. Belafonte was ex-military. I always suspected Rommel was, just by the way he carried himself."

"I thought Belafonte's fingerprints had been altered, like Rommel's."

"They had, but he had a pin in his leg. They traced the number back to a military hospital in Virginia. Belafonte was Casey Theriot. He was Special Forces and the military has been looking for him the last ten years."

Max whistled. "You thinking these guys were Special Forces who went rogue?"

"Rogue, mercenaries…doesn't really matter in the big scheme of things. The outcome is the same."

"What in the world have we stepped in the middle of?"

Holt frowned. "More importantly—how was our father involved and why was he murdered because of it?"

TANNER SPENT ANOTHER four frustrating hours trying to track the creature, but didn't find a trace of him on either side of the bank. It wasn't really surprising given the thick canopy of dead vines covering the ground, and it was also possible the creature hadn't come up the bank on that stretch of bayou at all.

Annoyed with the lost opportunity, he made his way back to where the crew was working, to see if Emmett Vernon had ever returned to do his job. The men were still hard at work on the fencing, and he gave Ray a nod as he entered the clearing.

Surprisingly, Vernon sat on a boulder making notes on a pad of paper. Tanner headed over and stood in front of the man, who continued to look down at the paper. Tanner's shadow fell right across his paper and he hadn't exactly tried to mask his approach. Vernon knew he was there. He was just choosing to ignore him.

"Emmett Vernon, right?" Tanner asked.

Vernon sighed and looked up at him, clearly disgusted. "Yeah, who's asking?"

"My name is Tanner LeDoux. Ms. Bettencourt has hired me to figure out who's vandalizing her property."

"Good luck with that," he said and dropped his gaze back to his paper.

"Any reason why I need luck?"

"Chasing legends in this swamp is going to require more than a good pair of boots."

"I'm a professional tracker."

Vernon froze and looked back up at him, his expression now wary. "You don't say."

"Yep. I grew up in the Mystere Parish swamps, got my degree in forestry and have worked as a game warden since college. I've never missed finding my target before, and I'm not about to start."

Vernon stared at him for a couple of seconds. "And you're telling me all this why, exactly?"

"Because I want information from you about what you think is going on."

"I would think it's obvious. A bunch of superstitious fools had some drinks on the job and imagined things."

Tanner glanced over at Ray, who was clearly angry at Vernon's words.

"It wasn't drunken superstition that tore down the fences," Tanner said.

"Right smart of you to figure that out. Now, what do you want from me?"

"Your thoughts on who might have enough of a problem to cause trouble."

"I already gave you my opinion on what happened, but you'll have to ask Josie who wants to cause her trouble."

"Josie can hardly have a beer with the locals and get them to talk, and being a stranger, neither can I."

Vernon scowled. "You want me to set up my friends and neighbors to pump them about something they ain't got nothing to do with? I don't think so."

"How do you know they're not involved?"

"Look. I don't know what Josie told you, but if someone's got a problem with her, I'd try looking into the people she met after she left Miel. She didn't come back here with her tail between her legs for no reason. You ask me, she's running from something. Maybe you should ask her if it came looking for her."

A flash of anger passed over Tanner at the way Vernon spoke about Josie. "That's a hard line to take about your employer, isn't it? Haven't you worked for the family for years?"

"I worked for her father, not Josie."

"Well, it appears to me that Josie is the one signing

your paychecks now. I'll expect you to show her a little more respect in the future."

The crew had already slowed, but when Tanner delivered that statement, all work ceased completely. A red flush crept up Vernon's neck and across his face. He stood, his face inches from Tanner, glaring at him.

"I expect you to do the job you were hired to do," Vernon said, "and not worry about how I do mine." He shot an angry look at the crew, then stomped off into the swamp toward the house.

Tanner watched his retreating back and contemplated going after him for a couple of seconds. Finally, he decided it wasn't worth it, but he knew Josie would likely be hurt and offended at the way the foreman had spoken about her.

He looked over at the crew, and all the men except Ray looked down at the ground. Ray looked as if he wanted to say something but only waved at the crew to get back to work. Tanner sighed and started toward the trail that led back to the house. He'd gotten about twenty yards down it when he heard someone behind him. He turned around and saw Ray hurrying up the trail.

"Mr. LeDoux," Ray said. "I shouldn't be speaking to you about this, as Vernon is my boss, but I agree that what he said about Ms. Bettencourt is disrespectful. Disrespecting ladies don't sit right with me."

Tanner nodded. "I'm guessing being accused of being drunk on the job doesn't sit well with you, either. It wouldn't me."

"No, sir, it doesn't, so I'm going to say something I wouldn't otherwise. I don't trust the man."

Tanner stared, a bit surprised at the man's directness. "Any particular reason why?"

"He disappears most of the day. I know he's supposed

to be helping with the work. I've heard Ms. Bettencourt say as much, but he's never here more than a couple of minutes before he disappears into the swamp."

"Any idea what he does out there?"

"No, but I've never see him with fish or game, so I can only assume he's up to no good. Ain't no man needs to walk around in the swamp all day to clear his mind."

"That's true."

"I followed him a bit one day, but I think he heard me." Ray gave Tanner a sheepish look. "He lost me in the undergrowth."

"We all lose the trail sometimes."

"Yessir, but I don't very often. Vernon's good…real good. I'm just letting you know, in case you had in mind to see what he's up to."

"I appreciate it. Hey, what time did he come back to the work site today?"

"About two hours ago."

"And he didn't say anything about where he'd been or what he was doing?"

"Nope." Ray frowned. "It was kinda strange, though. He was soaking wet. Like he'd been swimming or something. He's stayed at the site longer today than he has since I started, but he still didn't lift a finger to help. He only sat there scribbling on that paper of his."

"I appreciate you telling me all this."

"I don't like to talk about another man's business," Ray said, "but I don't think Vernon is doing right by Ms. Bettencourt. She's worried about everything opening on time, and Vernon shouldn't be adding to that worry."

"You're right. It's his job to eliminate some of that worry. If you hear or observe anything else that looks off, please let me know."

"I will. Are you staying at the main house?"

"Until I find the vandal, yes."

"That's good. I don't think Ms. Bettencourt should be there alone. I have to tell you that if this job was for anyone but Ms. Bettencourt, I would have quit already. I got a bad feeling about all of this." He gave Tanner a nod and headed back down the path to the work site.

Tanner watched as he walked away. He had a bad feeling, as well.

THE VANDAL WATCHED the tracker and the crew leader from behind a cypress tree. Only pieces of the conversation carried to the cypress tree, but it was easy to fill in the gaps. They were both worried about the bitch. The simpering, whining, spoiled bitch. The crew leader was of no concern. The man didn't have the nerve or the skill to follow someone with considerable skill through the swamp, but the tracker was worrisome.

On the plus side, the crew men were nervous and superstitious. The easiest way to shut down all this nonsense was to scare them off the job. Strong, available men weren't exactly plentiful, and even fewer wanted to work in the swamp when they could get higher-paying work in the midst of the sights and thrills of New Orleans.

Tonight, the vandal would strike again.

Chapter Seven

Josie had showered and changed and was standing in front of the refrigerator when Tanner walked in the back door. The sun was already setting, casting a dim glow over the back lawn. She felt her lower back loosen as she saw him walk inside and realized how tense she'd been, wondering what he'd found, if anything.

"I was just trying to decide on supper," she said. "I'm afraid I don't have much in stock, but I could fry some bacon and eggs if you're interested."

Tanner pulled off his gloves and set them on the counter. He looked as if he was thinking hard on something, and she was dying to know what it was.

"Actually," he said, "I wondered if you'd be interested in having dinner in town, and maybe a beer?"

A twinge of excitement passed over her, and she chided herself. The seriousness of his expression let her know the invitation was not personal, which was the last thing she needed at the moment, anyway.

"This invitation sounds like it comes with an agenda," she said.

"I'm afraid so. I want to get out into town. Watch the locals and see if I can stir up some talk."

"And get the word spread around that I have a tracker living on the property."

He nodded. "It will either shut him down or cause him to escalate. When people rush, they tend to make mistakes, so if he escalates, I'm depending on him getting sloppy enough for me to catch him."

"So I guess that means you didn't find anything today?"

He frowned and Josie got the immediate impression she wasn't going to like what he was about to say.

"I had a talk with Emmett Vernon," he said and told her the details of the conversation.

A flush ran up her face and she clenched her hands. The nerve of the man who'd made a good living off her family, talking about her that way.

"I don't know what Emmett is trying to imply, but I promise you, there are no skeletons that followed me back to Miel. Those people only care about the fashion world, and tucked away in the swamp, I am hardly a threat to models vying for the same gig."

"I didn't figure, but I wanted you to be aware of what he's saying. Your crew leader was a bit upset about it, too."

"Ray is a good man. I'm sorry he's in the middle of all this drama. He has a nice family to support and just wants to do his job."

Tanner nodded. "He told me he doesn't trust Vernon. Men like Ray don't say those kinds of things lightly, especially to a stranger."

She blew out a breath. "No, I suppose not. So, what do we do?"

"You go about your business as usual. I'm going to fish around into Vernon's business a bit and see if anything surfaces."

"This is all just so distressing. The man was like an

uncle to me, and all of a sudden, it's like I don't know him at all."

"We'll figure it out. Vernon may have reasons for his behavior that have nothing to do with this situation. He's not exactly the kind of man who would lay his problems out at your feet."

"No, I guess he's not."

"There's something else," he said.

One look at his face had her back tightening again. "Why do I get the feeling I'm *really* not going to like this?"

"Because I don't like it, either." He blew out a breath. "I saw what you saw. I chased it through the swamp, but lost it in the bayou. I couldn't find the place where he climbed back up the bank."

She stared for a couple of seconds, not even breathing. "You saw it?"

"Only a little, but it was exactly as you described."

"Do you still think it's a man in a suit?"

"That makes the most sense. Someone familiar with the swamp would have known how to ditch me."

"And that's why you want to observe the locals."

"Yeah."

He stared down at the counter again, and her antenna went up.

"You're not leaving anything out, are you?" she asked.

He blew out a breath and looked back up at her. "Thing is, I saw it over a section of brush."

"Okay?" She wasn't quite getting the problem.

"That brush was a good six feet high."

She sucked in a breath and looked out the windows

and into the swamp. It looked so peaceful, but something lurked out there. What was it?

The even bigger question—what did it want?

TANNER STEPPED OUT OF the shower and dried off with one of the huge fluffy towels. The towels in his apartment were thin, scratchy and covered with bare spots. He supposed that was one of the advantages to having women around, they knew how to make things comfortable and paid attention to details.

Still, buying new towels was a lot cheaper and held far less irritation than a relationship, so he supposed a trip to the store was on his list of things to do when he was done with the case. Maybe he'd spring for new sheets and blankets, too. The current ones almost matched his towels.

He pulled on jeans, a shirt and boots, and ran a brush through his damp hair. He considered putting on cologne, but then remembered he hadn't brought any with him. It was just as well, as cologne might make it look too much like a date. The last thing he wanted was to make things personal. Seeing Josie every day, especially so worried, was harder than he'd imagined, and he'd imagined damned hard. This was worse.

Every time he looked at her, he wanted to pull her into his arms and tell her it would all work out fine. Then his thoughts drifted to less honorable actions.

He shook his head, trying to clear his mind of thoughts of Josie in his arms. It wasn't going to happen now any more than it had happened when they were teens. He was just as out of his depth as before. She was the world-traveled high-fashion model who'd inherited a family fortune and owned expensive horses. He was just the local boy with a cheating father and drunken mother who spent all his time staring at mud.

Those two planes would never meet. She had no reason to lower herself to live on his, and he could never get himself high enough to match hers.

His cell phone rang and he answered Holt's call.

"I got that information you requested," his brother said. "Everyone's clean except Mack Prevet. He was arrested on an assault charge about eight years ago when he was running a bar in New Orleans."

"You get any details on that?"

"Yeah, I talked to the arresting officer. He says Prevet got into a fight with his live-in girlfriend at the bar and clocked her in the face. She refused to press charges, but there were a dozen witnesses in the bar."

"Sounds like a nice guy."

"Oh, yeah, and apparently one that has no problem terrorizing women. He's also in the red with his bar in Miel. Has it hocked to the gills. Rumor has it, he has a bit of a gambling problem."

"Thanks for the information. I'm going to get an up-close and personal look at him tonight." He told Holt about his plans for dinner and drinks in Miel, hoping to pick up some information on the locals and perhaps flush out the vandal.

"Be careful," Holt said. "If you spook him, he may escalate. Is Josie okay with this plan?"

"Yes. We discussed it earlier and she knows the risks involved."

"Well, in that case, enjoy your dinner with a beautiful woman."

Tanner could practically see his brother smiling as he delivered that last comment, but Tanner wasn't about to take the bait. "I will," he said, and disconnected.

He stepped out of his room at the same time as Josie walked out of hers. One look at her and he felt his chest tighten. He'd seen her on the cover of magazines, wearing clothes that probably cost more than he made in a year, but standing in the hallway in jeans, a blue top and black heels, she looked more gorgeous than ever.

Critics had been fond of saying that her auburn hair was her downfall to greatness, that if she'd been a blonde, she could have hit the big time. Tanner didn't know anything about the modeling big time, nor did he normally go around describing hair as "auburn," but he knew they were wrong. Her hair fell in waves across her shoulders, gently framing her face and making her green eyes stand out even more.

"Is something wrong?" she asked.

Yanking himself out of his stupor, he said, "Not at all. Actually, I was just thinking about how going to dinner might not be the best idea."

Her face fell and she tugged at the hem of her blouse. "Oh, okay."

"Because I might have to fight off every man who sees you." He smiled. "You look great."

She broke out in a smile that almost blinded him. "Thank you. That's the best compliment I've heard in a while."

"I find that hard to believe."

She waved a hand in dismissal. "Stop or you're going to make my head swell. I'm starving. Shall we?"

He gestured to the stairs. "My pickup truck awaits your pleasure."

She started down the stairwell. "Aside from my horses, you're likely to be the best company I've had in years."

He laughed and followed her outside. "That's some

good company, putting me up against the horses." He opened the passenger door of his truck and she climbed inside.

"I meant to ask you about the horses last night," he said after he climbed in the driver's seat and started up the road to town. "Things were kind of crazy and I forgot. They're Arabians, right?"

"Yes. I met a breeder on a shoot in France. His horses were magnificent. I'd never seen anything so majestic. We stayed at his ranch several weeks and I spent every spare moment shadowing him and watching him work with the horses. I'd helped my dad break and train quarter horses before, but this was different."

"You were already planning on getting some?"

"Not then. I mean, I wanted one more than anything, but it wouldn't have been possible at the time. My job was too demanding, and I was rarely in one place long enough to keep a cactus alive, much less care for and train a horse."

"So you got them when you came home?"

She nodded. "I got really lucky. The breeder I'd met in France had a friend in the States who was retiring from the business. He'd had a heart attack and wanted to spend his remaining years on a beach and not in a barn."

"Not a bad plan."

"If you can afford it, it's a great plan."

Tanner glanced over at her, confused by her tone. Franklin Bettencourt had been king of Miel, and Josie was his only child. Between her inheritance and what she must have made modeling, she should be able to buy a small island.

"Probably not in my future, then," he said. For whatever reason, Josie wanted to pretend she wasn't wealthy. Maybe it embarrassed her, or maybe she thought he'd jack up the price if he knew what she was worth. He looked out the dashboard down the narrow road. None of it was his business. He needed to stick with the case and stop running off down rabbit trails.

"So I guess you got some horses from the guy who retired?" he asked.

"Yes. The breeder in France called and spoke to him. He gave me a really good deal because he knew Raul would help me with the training."

Tanner frowned. So it was Raul now. He wondered just how close Josie and the French horse breeder had become. He'd seen no pictures of Josie with a man in the house, but he hadn't been in her bedroom, either. And being in a different country, she was likely calling him at a time when he wasn't around to overhear.

None of it's your business.

The repeating thought flashed through his mind again, then another came—*to hell with it.*

"So are you and Raul…"

"What? Oh…no!" She laughed. "Raul lives with a very nice man named Jacques."

"Ahhhh," he said, not able to form a coherent reply to such an unexpected answer.

"I vowed off relationships a long time ago," she said. "Besides, I have more than enough to keep me busy. No time for much else. What about you?"

"Me?"

"Yeah, you. You must have your share of admirers."

"I spend most of my time in the swamp. It's not exactly the best place to find a date, and I prefer it that way."

"Well, then I guess both of us are outside our comfort zone tonight."

"I guess so," he said, not sure what to make of her

comment. He'd been clear that tonight was about business, not personal. Likely, he was overthinking it. Thank goodness his brothers couldn't read his mind. He probably wouldn't look near as good a bet for a business partner as they thought. Certainly he didn't have his life together like the two of them.

He held in a sigh as he pulled into town and parked in front of the only restaurant open for dinner. All his life, he'd been running to catch up to his older brothers. He'd hoped once they reached adulthood that things would change, but here he was, still comparing himself to Holt and Max and coming up short.

He looked over at Josie, who hadn't moved from the passenger's seat, and was staring at the restaurant with an apprehensive look. "So, is the food any good here?" he asked.

"It used to be," she said. "I've only eaten here once since I've returned home, but it was good then. Not much for variety, but if you're a burger, ribs or steak guy, then I think you'll be fine."

"Add a beer and that's the four food groups," he joked.

She smiled and he saw her shoulders relax a bit, which was what he'd been hoping to accomplish. If she looked nervous, people might clue in to the fact that it wasn't just a friendly dinner. If people thought ulterior motives were at play, they might not talk.

"Let's get inside and get some dinner," he said. "I'm starving."

They climbed out of the truck and made their way into the restaurant. Tanner was surprised to see most of the tables were full, but they were quickly escorted to a table in the back of the room.

"It's busy," Tanner said as he took a seat. "I guess that's a good sign that the food is edible."

"Or that people are too busy or too lazy to cook."

He laughed. "Yeah, there is that."

As the hostess took their drink orders, Tanner took the opportunity to scan the room. The general volume had decreased when he'd walked in with Josie. He'd expected as much. He was a stranger and he was with the local town princess. People were bound to be curious. In fact, he was counting on that curiosity to loosen lips.

When the hostess left, he leaned in toward Josie. "So, give me a rundown of some of the people here."

She nodded. "Anyone in particular you want to start with?"

"The guy at the table up front with the red shirt on hasn't stopped staring at you since we walked in. What's his story?"

She took a sip of water, glanced at the front of the restaurant, then frowned. "That's Sam Walker. Local real estate agent, huge gossip and general pest."

He held in a smile. "So I take it you like him?"

"I went to school with him, as I did with most every adult in Miel under the age of forty. He didn't know how to shut up then and he still doesn't."

Tanner nodded. Although he hadn't spent much time attending school, he had a vague recollection of overhearing Sam's verbal tirades more than once. Josie had nailed this one.

Josie studied Tanner for a moment, then grinned. "He called the house this afternoon and asked me out."

"Oh?"

"Yeah. I told him I wasn't interested in dating. He probably had a coronary when I walked in with you. He would never believe he's not the best catch in town."

Tanner gave Sam a sideways glance. He couldn't blame the man for trying but had to admit, he liked him even less than before when he was just some dude with a rude staring problem. "Don't look now, but I think he's coming over to clarify your policy on dating."

Her look of dismay left no doubt of her feelings about the Realtor, and he felt a smug sense of satisfaction.

"Josie," Sam said as he stepped up to the table. "I'm surprised to see you out. I thought you were too busy for socializing."

Josie looked up at him, her face the perfection of politeness. "Hi, Sam." She waved a hand at Tanner. "This is Tanner LeDoux. He's helping me with a situation concerning the construction."

Sam looked over at Tanner and gave him a fake smile as he extended his hand. "Sam Walker. Nice to meet you."

Tanner shook his hand, squeezing it just a bit harder than necessary, and feeling an inordinate amount of satisfaction when the man flinched before releasing his hand.

"So you're in construction? So am I, of sorts. I own the real estate agency in town."

Tanner shook his head. "I'm not in construction."

Sam looked expectantly at him, clearly waiting for an explanation, but Tanner just stared back at him. Finally, it got the best of the man and he asked, "So, what is it you do, then?"

"That's Ms. Bettencourt's business. I'm not at liberty to say."

"He's a tracker," Josie said. "Looking into the vandalism problems for me."

Sam's eyes widened. "Well, I guess you meant it earlier when you said you'd be opening on time. I suppose a tracker won't have any trouble finding the bear responsible for the damage."

"Or the man," Tanner said.

Sam yanked his head back in Tanner's direction, his jaw set. "I'm not sure what you're implying, but the only people who know that swamp well enough to escape detection are people who live here in Miel. None of them would take kindly to being accused of vandalism."

"Well, I guess if none of them are doing it, then they don't have a problem, do they?"

Sam looked back at Josie. "Do you really want to alienate the people in this town even more?" He shook his head. "I wish you'd consider my offer. It's a good price. More than enough money for you to buy a new facility for your horses."

Tanner saw a flush creep up Josie's neck.

"I've already told you," she said, her voice clipped, "that my family home is not for sale."

Knowing he'd been defeated, Sam held his hands up in surrender. "Hey, I'm just giving you an option. If you ever change your mind about any of this," he said, and glanced over at Tanner, "you know where to find me."

He didn't even acknowledge Tanner before he walked away. Tanner could tell by the stiff set in his shoulders that the Realtor wasn't happy about the exchange.

"What's he talking about?" Tanner asked. "Someone wants to buy your property?"

Josie, who'd been watching Sam's retreating back, turned to look at Tanner. "I guess so."

"Has he pressured you at all?"

"No." She frowned. "Why?"

Tanner shrugged. "I was just thinking if someone wanted the property badly enough, they might try to scare you off it."

"I don't know of any reason someone would want it that badly."

"Oil, maybe? Have you had a study done?"

"No, but that wouldn't matter. No one in these parts lets the mineral rights go when they sell."

"That's true enough. All the same, it's something to keep an eye on."

A young woman with short brown hair stepped up to the table. "Are you ready to order?" she asked, looking directly at Tanner.

"Ladies first," he said, and gestured to Josie.

The girl hesitated a second, then looked over at Josie. "What can I get for you?"

"I'll take the Cajun chicken dinner with steamed vegetables, please," she said, then looked up at the woman.

"Salad or soup?"

Josie's brow wrinkled as she studied the waitress. "Marquette?"

The waitress frowned. "Yeah?"

"I'm Josie Bettencourt. I remember you from high school."

Tanner took a hard look at the waitress, but no bells went off.

Marquette studied Josie for a moment, then nodded. "I remember you now. You were a couple years ahead of me."

Josie nodded. "Your brother Rob was in my class. How is he?"

"Good. He went into the Marines. Has a wife and a daughter."

"How nice." Josie smiled. "Please tell him I said hello the next time you talk to him."

"Sure."

"Oh, gosh, I'm being rude," Josie said, and waved a

hand at Tanner. "This is Tanner LeDoux. He's a tracker helping me with some vandalism I've had at my house."

Marquette glanced at Tanner.

"Nice to meet you," Tanner said.

"You, too," she murmured, then continued to stand there, staring at Josie.

"I'm so sorry. I never answered you," Josie said. "I'll take the soup please."

The girl made a note on her pad, then took Tanner's order of ribs, mashed potatoes and rolls. Josie watched as she walked away from the table.

"Is there a problem?" Tanner asked.

"What— No." Josie looked back at him. "It's just that I haven't seen her since she was a kid, really. I guess she was a late bloomer. I almost didn't recognize her."

"She didn't seem overly friendly."

"She was always quiet…you know, the odd kid who sat in the corner at parties."

"Was her brother the same way?"

"Heavens, no. Rob was our star wide receiver and prom king. He was the most outgoing, friendly person you could ever meet."

Suddenly, a memory of Rob Pitre flashed through his mind. He remembered the talented running back all the girls were crazy about. With all the moving around, Tanner had eventually given up on making friends, but even if he had tried, Rob's group wouldn't have been accessible to him. They were all jocks and from the best families in town.

He tried to remember if Josie had ever dated him, but couldn't ever recall seeing them together, except in a newspaper picture of them as Prom King and Queen. He also remembered Rob as being friendly and polite, completely unlike the annoying Sam.

He racked his brain for a memory of Rob's sister, but came up empty. Apparently, Josie was right in saying she'd been a quiet one. Tanner usually noticed everyone. Even as a teen, he'd been more inclined to sit and observe than to get in the mix, but Marquette didn't register anywhere in his mind. He glanced over at the window where the waitresses were putting in their orders to get another look at Marquette and caught her staring directly at them, frowning.

He yanked his gaze back to Josie, who was unfolding her napkin and hadn't even noticed the exchange. "Looks like we've accomplished our goal," he said. "Don't look now, but Marquette is giving us the once-over."

"You think she'll talk?"

"Yeah, and she's in the perfect position to let everyone who comes in here know what she finds out. After dinner, we'll head next door to the bar. I'd be willing to bet that by morning, everyone in Miel will know you've hired a tracker to catch the vandal."

"That or they'll think I'm using it as a cover for living in sin." She rolled her eyes. "Small towns. Bible Belt."

He grinned. "It would be a shame to let all that talk happen and not get any benefit from it."

She smiled. "And what makes you so sure that sleeping with you would be a benefit?"

"I wasn't talking about you."

Her mouth dropped open just a bit and a flush ran up her neck. "Do you always hit on the clients?"

"I don't know. You're my first. I guess we'll have to wait and see if they're all as stunning as you."

Josie stared at him, apparently unable to formulate a good comeback. Out of the corner of his eye, he saw the door to the restaurant swing open and Emmett Vernon walked past on the sidewalk as a little silver-haired lady walked inside.

"Take a minute to come up with a good retort," he said. "I'll be back before the food gets here."

Before she could respond, he jumped up from the table and hurried out of the restaurant to follow Vernon.

Chapter Eight

Josie stared after Tanner, completely taken aback by his clear attraction to her and his abrupt departure. What in the world was going on with that man? For the first time since her modeling years, she felt as if she were in a whirlwind. It wasn't a feeling she'd ever wanted to repeat. Control was much more preferable.

"Josie, are you all right?" Adele's voice broke into her thoughts and she realized her friend was standing right next to her table, and she hadn't even noticed her approach.

"Adele, hi. Yes, I'm fine. I was just lost in thought."

Adele patted her hand. "That happens to the best of us, dear." She looked over at the empty place across from her. "I saw a very nice-looking gentleman hurry out of here. He didn't say something to offend you, did he?"

Josie smiled. "Not at all. In fact, he'd just finished hitting on me when he rushed out. I have no idea why."

"No idea why he hit on you, or no idea why he rushed out? If it's the first, I say it's because you look very beautiful tonight and he's not blind. I've got no idea on the rushing off part. Who is he? One of those model friends of yours?"

She frowned. "I didn't make any friends modeling.

Certainly, some pretended to be, but there were no real relationships formed during my brief career." It was a shame it had taken her so long to realize that painful truth.

"Well, he's certainly handsome enough to be in a magazine."

"Yes, I suppose he is."

Adele laughed and wagged her finger at Josie. "Don't even sit there and pretend to me, young lady, that you haven't noticed an attractive young man who's hitting on you. Why, if I were thirty years younger, I'd take a run at him myself."

"Thirty years?"

"Okay, fifty."

Josie grinned, then leaned toward Adele and lowered her voice. "The reality is Mr. LeDoux's good looks are not relevant at all, although I'm certainly not complaining about the view. The fact is, he's only here because of you. Tanner is the private investigator you're paying for."

Adele broke out into a smile. "Really? Well, that's great news."

"He's also a professional tracker, which is quite a handy combination given my problems."

"Has he found out anything?"

"No, but he only started yesterday. Mostly, he's been poking around." She sighed. "And unfortunately, that started with looking into the background of all the workers, including Emmett."

Adele shook her head. "I don't imagine Emmett will take kindly to someone poking into his private business, but I can see why Tanner thinks he needs to do so."

"It's not just him being thorough." She told Adele

about her problems with the longtime foreman, especially his daily disappearing act.

"What do you think is going on?" Adele asked, clearly worried.

"I have no earthly idea. Maybe nothing at all to do with me or the construction, but he's acting weird, and there's got to be a reason for it. He's not exactly giving Tanner a reason to take him off his radar."

"No. Tanner wouldn't be doing his job if he didn't connect all the dots. Is he staying at your house while he's investigating?"

"Yes, although I'm not exactly comfortable with the idea. I mean, I like having someone to rely on right there, but at the same time, living with another man wasn't on my list of things to do."

"Especially one you're attracted to."

Josie sighed. "Okay, yes, he's totally hot."

"And?"

"And nice, and interesting and a gentleman. All of which is irrelevant."

Adele shook her head. "I know you've had a lot to deal with since your daddy got ill and it's only gotten more complicated, but try not to let too much life pass you by before you start living it again, instead of just walking through it."

Adele leaned over to kiss Josie's forehead and then crossed the restaurant to join her friends.

Josie glanced at the empty seat across from her and signaled to Marquette. Suddenly, a drink sounded like a really good idea. She'd been given entirely too much to think about before dinner.

TANNER CROSSED THE STREET several buildings up from the general store. Vernon lived at a cabin on Josie's property, but there were a hundred good reasons for him to be in town that evening. Tanner simply wanted to make sure that whatever he was doing fell on that list.

He walked up the sidewalk toward the general store, slowing as he approached the plate-glass windows that composed the storefront. Not wanting to draw attention to himself standing there, he pulled his cell phone out of his pocket and pretended to be on a call. He shuffled a bit in place and glanced around, appearing to be looking at nothing, but a quick peek inside the store got him a clear view of Vernon, standing at the back counter talking to a clerk.

He put the cell phone back in his pocket and strolled into the store, taking an immediate right behind one of the many shelves of canned goods. Over the top of the rows, he could just make out the back of Vernon's head. He was still standing at the counter.

If he went to the end of the row, he'd be able to get to the row of goods immediately behind the counter. It might be close enough to overhear their conversation. Silently, he edged down the end of the rows and slid down the last row until he was directly behind Vernon and the clerk. He positioned himself directly in front of a shelf that had a cardboard advertisement on top of it that blocked the top of his head perfectly.

"Ted, the girl's lost her mind," Vernon said.

"Now," Ted said, "she's young and she just lost her dad. Lost her mother years before that. You know how close they all were. Can't be easy on her."

"I'm not a total heel. I know the girl's hurting, but she's making some damned foolish decisions. How in the world she can even think about having a bunch of strangers living in her house, coming in and out like they was using a revolving door, is beyond me."

"Maybe she needs the money. There's rumors that Franklin wasn't doing all that well before he died. His medical bills couldn't have been cheap, either."

"It would take a lot more than heart surgery to bankrupt Franklin Bettencourt." Vernon sighed. "Maybe you're right. Maybe she's not as flush as I thought she'd be, but she had to have made some good money modeling. Franklin was always showing me a magazine with her picture in it."

"Maybe she spent it all. You see that kind of thing on the news all the time. Those young people, making all that money and putting it straight up their nose."

"That don't sound much like Josie, but I guess none of us really know what she did overseas. What I do know is she's come back with some bad ideas that are getting worse. You heard we had some trouble with the fences, right?"

"Yep," Ted said. "Sheriff Reynard was in here the other day, bragging about how he told her that what the wildlife did on private property wasn't his concern."

"The man's a jackass, but he's not wrong."

"You figure it's a bear?"

"Of course it is. That's still a problem, but it's not a police matter."

"You gonna track him?"

"Oh, that's the best part," Vernon replied. "I don't have to. Josie's gone and hired a professional tracker to find the problem critter. She's done moved him into the house and everything."

"She's paying a professional to track a bear? Hell, my ten-year-old grandson could track a bear. They ain't all that sneaky."

"I don't think Josie believes it's a bear. I think she believes that bunch of superstitious swamp men working on the crew. They think they saw the Tainted Keitre."

"Be good for business if they had, and I could use an uptick here. Might get more tourists this way instead of all of them flocking to New Orleans."

"You know as well as I do it's a load of hooey. They were either drunk or managed to spook themselves."

"You're probably right," Ted agreed. "Still, doesn't seem to be no harm in Josie hiring a tracker to put the whole thing to rest, and it saves you the hassle of dealing with it."

"Says you. He came out to the job site today to play twenty questions with me. I don't appreciate some stranger asking me to explain myself and my job. Ain't none of his business, no matter what he's paid to do."

"What's he talking to you for? You ain't seen anything, have you?"

"No. I got the impression he thinks it's a man, not a bear, doing the damage."

"Could he be right?"

"Sure, a man coulda tore down them fences," Vernon said. "But I'm betting on bear. Why would a man waste time tearing down fences in the swamp on private property? It seems a lot of effort just to delay the inevitable. Josie's determined to go through with turning her house into a hotel."

"Well, he ain't gonna make any friends around Miel if he starts peeking up skirts and treating people like suspects."

"That's his problem, I guess. I just hope he gets it handled and leaves soon."

"From what you say, it would probably be best for everyone," Ted said. "What about that other thing we talked about?"

"No word yet, but I'll let you know."

"I hope it works out. That could be a really good deal for me and Annie. Business hasn't been all that great for a couple of years. I gotta find other ways to make ends meet."

"I know," Vernon said. "As soon as I hear back from the guy in New Orleans, you'll be the first to know."

"I appreciate it. You need any supplies while you're here?"

"Yeah, give me a couple boxes of bullets for my pistol."

"You thinking you might run into trouble over this?" Ted asked, his voice strained.

"You never know what might come up in the swamp. Best to be prepared."

Tanner heard some shuffling and the ring of the cash register. He hustled to the end of the row and slid behind a display of handbags just as Vernon walked past the row and out of the store. Tanner peered over the top of the row and saw Ted step from behind the counter to assist a customer with a saddle in the back of the store.

The saddles were located on one side of the store, blocking Ted's view of the entry, so he hurried down the rows, cast a quick glance at the street to make sure it was clear then eased out of the store and down the block.

What are Vernon and the store owner up to? It was something in the swamp that was worth two boxes of bullets to protect and would help Ted make ends meet. Put together, it didn't look pretty.

He wondered if his presence had prompted the stocking up on bullets. If so, that wasn't good. Whatever Vernon was up to, it was clear Josie didn't know about it. The connection in New Orleans troubled him most of all. Vernon was involved in something that required partnerships with people in the city—secret partnerships.

There were a lot of things that came to his mind, especially after spending the past decade in the swamps. Drug running was the first.

And the most dangerous.

DINNER WAS SURPRISINGLY enjoyable for Josie. Tanner had returned to the table just before the food was served, but when she'd asked about his absence, he'd glanced around and then shook his head. Whatever he'd gone out for, he either wasn't sharing or wasn't sharing it in public.

So they'd talked about normal things like politics, sports and current events. She would have liked to find out more about the mysterious tracker, but every time she wandered into personal territory, he changed the subject or put the question back on her. By the end of dinner, she still didn't know a single thing about Tanner's personal life or his past that she hadn't known before walking in the restaurant.

A big strike against him, regardless of Adele's advice.

If she couldn't trust a man, she couldn't trust herself with him. Not even for a fling. She couldn't risk being made a fool of again, especially not in her hometown. At least, her past embarrassment had occurred a continent away. She was the only one in Miel who knew about it, and it was going to remain that way.

In Miel, she didn't get the looks of pity that some had for her, or the looks of disdain from others who felt she was a fool for being played. Here she was just Josie Bettencourt, hometown girl. No one knew about her past mistakes, and she wasn't about to make them again.

Tanner LeDoux, with his flirting and subsequent secrecy, was a prime candidate for a meltdown later on. Whatever slim thought she'd had about letting down her guard was gone from her mind by the time they finished eating.

Despite the fact that they were technically "working," he insisted on paying for dinner, which confused Josie even more. Finally, she decided it was either good upbringing, pride or both that prevented him from letting her foot the bill. He gave Marquette a nice tip and thanked her before leaving. She gave him a shy smile but glanced away almost immediately.

Josie briefly wondered why Marquette had chosen a profession like waitressing when she was clearly so uncomfortable around people, but then she reminded herself that options weren't all that plentiful in Miel and moving to New Orleans was probably more of a strain than the withdrawn young woman could handle.

Tanner looked over at her as they walked down the street to the bar. "Are you ready for round two?"

"I suppose so, especially as round one was rather uneventful."

He nodded. "Yeah, but the restaurant pulls a different crowd than the bar. I wanted as many people talking as possible. Besides, I was hungry and the ribs were excellent."

She laughed. "You're right on all counts. I haven't had a meal that good in months. I've been so busy, I rarely leave the house, and I'm not much for cooking. I figure a sandwich does me fine, and there's more important things to do with my time."

"I'm the same way. Unless friends harass me into a meal, I rarely get a great one. I'm surprised you don't meet friends in town. You can't work all the time."

"Most of the people I considered casual friends years ago have moved away. There's not a lot here to offer young people looking to establish themselves. I do go visit Adele sometimes. She's the little silver-haired lady who walked in the restaurant when you were leaving. She was a good friend of my mom's—started off as her babysitter."

"So she's essentially family, just not by blood."

"Yeah, I guess she is. I've never thought about it that way, but you're right." She smiled. "So I guess I'm not alone, after all."

"It's tough not having your parents around, especially if you were close."

Something in his tone made her wonder if his words weren't only about her. Even though she figured he'd find a way around her question, she still had to ask, "Are your parents still around?"

"No. I lost my dad when I was eight. My mom died my first year of college."

Her heart ached for him, losing both parents at such a young age. Instantly, she felt guilty for being so harsh on him for not talking about his personal life. It had never crossed her mind that the memories could be mostly painful.

"I'm sorry," she said. "I can't imagine how hard that was. I feel sorry for myself losing my parents so young, but at least I was well into adulthood before either of them passed. You had your brothers, though. There's three of you, right?"

"There's three of us, but I didn't really 'have' them. We all have different mothers."

"I didn't realize you were that far apart in age."

"We're not. Our father wasn't exactly the stuff good

husbands are made of. Holt and Max are only four months apart. I'm two years younger."

"Oh, wow," she said, mortified that she'd introduced this line of questioning. "I'm sorry. I didn't mean to bring up something painful."

He gave her a small smile. "You didn't. I got over what my dad did years ago. I didn't spend as much time with my brothers as Holt and Max spent together. They both lived in the same town. My mother moved us away after she figured out my dad wouldn't remain faithful to one woman. We moved back a time or two because she thought he'd changed, but we always ended up leaving again."

"That must have been hard on her."

"Probably, but she should have known better. He already had two sons by two different women, and from the rumors, the possibility existed for a lot more. She rolled the dice and came up short. After he died, I hoped we'd move back for good, but for whatever reason, my mother refused to go back to Vodoun. Instead, she hopped from one unfit Mystere Parish man to another."

Josie could tell by his tone that Tanner wasn't happy with his mother's choices. She couldn't really blame him. Her bad decision had left a little boy without a father, then she'd moved him away from his brothers.

"Holt's mom was the best, though," Tanner said. "She was happy to have us all at her house and treated Max and me like her own. No matter what our father put her through, she was always a class act."

The love that had been missing from his voice when talking about his own mother was so apparent when he spoke about Holt's. Also, she didn't miss the fact that he referred to one as "mother" and the other as "mom."

She guessed that Holt's mother had felt more like a mom to him than his own.

"She sounds like a wonderful woman. Is she still alive?"

"Alive and taking a much-deserved early retirement in Florida. I just visited her for a week last month."

He stopped suddenly and Josie realized they were in front of the bar. She choked back a bit of disappointment that their conversation ended so abruptly. Finally, she'd learned something beyond Tanner's résumé, and she'd been prevented from learning more by the length of the walk.

"Ready?" he asked.

She nodded and walked into the bar, wondering if she'd ever get the opportunity to delve into the inner workings of Tanner LeDoux again.

The bar was small and crowded. Tanner pointed to two empty stools at the bar and guided her through the maze of tables and people to take the two empty seats. A couple of seconds later, a big burly man came over to take their order.

"Beer." She almost had to yell above the noise in the bar.

Tanner held up two fingers. The man nodded and poured two beers from the tap in front of them, then slid them across the counter.

"Is that Mack Prevet?" Tanner asked.

"No," Josie said. "Mack's the one coming out of the storeroom and snarling."

"He's looking directly at you."

"Glaring is probably the least offensive thing he's done since I returned."

The bar owner locked in on Josie and Tanner and strode directly over to them.

"This ain't no photo shoot," Mack said. "You want to drink with your modeling buddies, you can do it at home."

Tanner laughed. "That's a new one. I've never been mistaken for a model before." He held out his hand to the scowling bar owner. "Tanner LeDoux. I'm a professional tracker. Josie hired me to stop the vandalism at her property."

Mack looked at Tanner's hand and then back up at him, not bothering to extend his hand. "Don't care who you are or what you're doing here, as long as you do it away from me."

Tanner lowered his hand. "I *was* away from you. You walked over here, remember?"

Mack narrowed his eyes at Tanner. "You've got a smart mouth on you, buddy. Go ahead and have your bit of fun with the ice princess, but if you get the least bit out of line in here, I'm throwing you out myself."

"Duly noted," Tanner said. "Hey, maybe when you have some time, we could talk about where you were the last two nights when someone was vandalizing Josie's property."

"Watch your step. Most men don't like being accused of things they haven't done."

"Did you take that as an accusation? That's interesting."

Mack glared at Tanner for a second, then stalked to the other end of the bar, where he leaned over to talk to a group of men gathered there.

"Word of my arrival is spreading fast," Tanner said, and nodded toward Mack.

"He certainly didn't like your implication."

"Yeah, maybe because he hasn't done anything

wrong. Maybe because he's the vandal. Hard to see the truth. That chip on his shoulder's blocking a lot."

"That man has serious issues," Josie said, shaking her head over the entire exchange. "So much drama for such a small place."

Tanner took a swig of his beer, then leaned in toward Josie. "Don't look now, but your friend Sam is on his way over—again."

She held in a groan as Sam stepped in between them.

"Josie," he said, without acknowledging Tanner at all, "I see you're making a full night of it. I feel badly about how I left things earlier. Let me make it up to you with a dance."

It was all Josie could do not to roll her eyes. The man actually thought dancing with him was a good thing.

"Actually," Tanner interrupted, and rose from his stool, "I'd just asked Josie to dance, so you'll have to take a number."

He extended his hand to Josie, who slipped off her stool and placed her hand in his. "Maybe next time, Sam," she said as she walked hand in hand with Tanner to the tiny, crowded dance floor.

The song was a slow one, and he pulled her in close to him, encircling her waist with his strong arms. She wrapped her arms around him, placing her hands flat on his back, her chest pressed against him. With her hands and her breasts, she could feel his toned, firm body, and she couldn't help wondering what it would look like in far less clothing. During her modeling days, she'd seen plenty of ripped males bodies in various stages of undress, but she'd bet her last dime that Tanner could give any of them a run for their money.

"Thank you for rescuing me from Sam," she said.

"It wouldn't have been very gentlemanly for me to

leave you stranded, listening to him for an entire song. You might have docked my pay."

She laughed. "I don't think this falls in the context of your job duties."

"That's a shame," he whispered as he pulled her closer. "If I was paid to do this, I'd probably never stop."

She laid her head against his chest and let out a sigh, all of her earlier resolve flying completely out the window. Only one other time had she met a man who could so easily turn her inside out.

And look how well that one worked out.

She bit her lower lip and tried to silently will herself into a mindless stupor. One dance wasn't going to hurt anything. If she couldn't enjoy a few minutes in the arms of a sexy man without it completely blowing her life plans, then she didn't have the backbone to carry them through in the first place.

Closing her eyes, she let herself melt into Tanner, swaying to the slow rhythm of the country tune playing on the jukebox. As he hummed along with the melody, the rest of the world drifted away and for a moment, all of her problems disappeared.

Chapter Nine

It was almost midnight when Tanner pulled up the driveway in front of the house. All of a sudden, he slammed on the brakes and killed the truck engine. Josie, who'd fallen half-asleep on the ride home, jerked into consciousness.

"What's wrong?" she asked.

"I saw a light in the upstairs window of my bedroom."

"Maybe you left it on."

"I'm sure I didn't, but even if I had, it still wouldn't be moving. This was small and mobile, probably from a flashlight."

He leaned across the truck and pulled his pistol and flashlight from his glove box.

"Stay here and lock the doors," he instructed.

"No—"

"You're safer here. We have no way of knowing how many of them are in there." He looked at his watch. "Give me five minutes, and if I don't return, drive straight back to Miel and get the sheriff."

Before she could say a word, he jumped out of the truck and eased the door closed, then hurried down the backside of a long row of hedges toward the house.

Josie leaned forward to stare out the windshield at the

house. Slowly, she scanned every window on the second floor, then the first, but she never saw even a flicker of light. She didn't doubt for a moment that Tanner had seen it, which meant that whoever was there had left or was hiding. Her mind struggled a bit, trying to decide which was the better option. If the intruder had left, then Tanner was not at risk, but if the intruder was still there and Tanner caught him, then it would all be over.

She looked at her watch and huffed out a breath when she realized not even a minute had passed. It already seemed like an eternity. A patch of clouds passed in front of the moon, and all the light extinguished. She sat in the pitch-black, unable even to make out the front of the truck. Her heartbeat echoed in her head and she realized that the swamp had gone completely silent.

Suddenly, she heard a crunch of leaves right outside her truck door, the tiny sound booming in the silent night. A wave of panic came over her and she reached for the door lock that she'd forgotten to press earlier. But before her fingers touched the button, the passenger door flew open and yellow eyes stared at her.

The creature growled and she screamed.

She tried to scramble across the seat, but the creature grabbed her and pulled her from the truck, wrapping one hairy arm around her waist and covering her mouth with his huge hand. She flailed about with everything she had, hands, arms, feet and legs, trying to tear loose, but the creature was too strong. He began to drag her into the swamp, and a second wave of panic hit her full force. Her heart beat so hard her chest ached from the effort.

Desperate to get away, she got her mouth on one of the creature's fingers and bit as hard as she could. The creature howled right in her ear and she thought her eardrum would split from the volume. He increased his speed, almost running as he dragged her along his side.

She closed her eyes to protect them from the dry foliage that scratched her face and bit him again as hard as she could. He yanked his hand from her mouth and she retched, gagging on the hair stuck in her throat. As soon as she could suck in a breath, she screamed again, her throat burning with the effort.

Suddenly, the creature released her and she fell to the ground. The last thing she remembered was her head striking something hard. Then everything went black.

JOSIE'S SCREAM RIPPED through the silence of the night air. Tanner's heart leaped into his throat as he tore downstairs and out the front door of the house, all thoughts of the intruder forgotten. He panicked when he saw the truck door standing open and Josie nowhere in sight. The thin glimmer of moonlight that was shining when he ran from the house faded away and left only the darkness in its place.

Stay calm.

He pulled out his flashlight and shined it on the ground next to the truck. The dirt right next to the truck showed clear signs of a struggle, so he cast the light to the surrounding area. A surge of panic ran through him when he saw the huge four-toed prints leading into the woods.

He had Josie!

Not even a second passed before Tanner launched into autopilot and followed the tracks into the swamp. The prints quickly disappeared on the canopy of dead leaves and vines, but the telltale signs of passage were there—broken branches, the occasional heel or toe print left in the tiny patches where the dirt was exposed.

He moved as quickly as he dared, knowing that making a mistake and having to backtrack could cost Josie her life.

A second scream tore through the swamp and he abandoned all concentration and ran directly toward the scream. The brush tore at his bare arms and face, but he didn't even pause, certain he was closing in on Josie.

A minute later, he tripped over a log and sprawled on the ground in a small clearing. He jumped to his feet, ready to take off again, but glanced back just in time to see that it wasn't a log he'd tripped over at all.

He rushed over to Josie's prone figure and knelt beside her, feeling for a pulse. A wave of relief passed over him as it pounded strong against his fingertips. Shining his light at her head, he saw a patch of blood and a cut. He had to get her inside.

He gathered her in his arms and hurried back down the path as quickly as possible, hoping all the while that her attacker had given up for the night. It wasn't possible to carry Josie and his pistol, and right now they were highly vulnerable. He tried to listen as he ran, but didn't hear the sounds of approaching prey.

He burst out of the swamp close to the barn, startling Emmett Vernon, who was standing outside the barn, smoking a cigarette.

"What the hell?" Vernon dropped his cigarette and ran up to Tanner.

"Josie was attacked. I've got to get her inside and call a doctor."

Vernon pulled out his pistol and dashed ahead of them and into the house. He flipped on the living room lights as Tanner hurried in and placed Josie on the couch. She was still unconscious and her face was so pale that a second wave of fear passed over Tanner.

"I'll call Doc Hebert," Vernon said, and grabbed the phone on the end table next to the couch. A couple of seconds later, he barked orders at the doctor and hung up the phone. "He's close by. Shouldn't take him but a couple of minutes to get here."

Tanner nodded and checked Josie's pulse again. It was still strong.

"Is she all right?" Vernon asked, the worry apparent in his voice.

"Her pulse is strong, but she's been unconscious since I found her."

Vernon ran one hand through his gray hair and paced the living room. "What the hell happened? I thought you were supposed to keep trouble away, not invite it to the damned house."

Tanner felt both angry and guilty at the other man's accusations. By advertising his purpose in Miel all over town that night, he *had* been inviting trouble. He just hadn't thought it would appear before they'd even gotten inside the house.

"I *was* protecting her. I saw a light in the house and told her to stay in the truck and go into town and get the sheriff if I didn't return in five minutes. I'd just gotten upstairs when I heard her scream and she was gone. I have no idea what happened."

Vernon's face turned red. "Running around town all night, flaunting what you were hired to do to everyone in Miel, is *protecting* her? I've had six phone calls about your little stunt already tonight. What the hell did you think was going to happen?"

"I thought he'd either go away or escalate. I was hoping for the first. I didn't expect the second so soon."

"Well, that's just great. I don't suppose you let Josie in on this fool plan of yours that almost got her killed?"

Tanner bristled and he struggled against the urge to punch Vernon squarely in the jaw. "Josie is aware and has approved everything I've done. I don't ignore my boss's wishes."

"Like me, you mean. Well, at least nothing I've done has put her in harm's way. You think about that one for a while. I'll wait for the doc out front. The air stinks in here."

Vernon gave Tanner one last disgusted look, then walked out the front door and into the driveway. Tanner sank down on the couch next to Josie and brushed a lock of her hair from her face.

He took a deep breath and blew it slowly out, trying to control his anger. Vernon had hacked him all the way off, but if he was being honest with himself, it was because what he'd said was true. This was all his fault. Josie had hired him because she wanted things to stop, not get worse. Now she'd been hurt, and it was killing him to sit here, waiting on the doctor and not knowing if she was going to be all right.

He was just about to suck up his pride and ask Vernon to call the doctor's house again when she stirred, then groaned softly.

"Josie?" He leaned in closer to her, studying her face.

Her eyelids flickered a couple of times, then flew open and she tried to jump up from the couch. He held her shoulders with both hands and prevented her from rising.

"It's Tanner," he said as her eyes flashed wildly back and forth across the room. "You're safe in your own living room."

Her eyes locked on his and she slumped back down on the couch. "I'm so sorry. I forgot to lock the truck doors and then there was a noise outside. I tried to lock them but he'd already pulled open the door."

He leaned down toward her. "Who? Who pulled open the door?"

She stared at him, her eyes wide. "The Tainted Kietre. He dragged me out of the truck and into the swamp. I fought like crazy, and even bit him. That's why he finally dropped me."

"It must have been a man in a suit."

She shook her head. "He was huge with yellow eyes, and the smell…"

Tanner felt his lower back tighten. "What kind of smell?"

She scrunched her brown in concentration. "Like a skunk, sort of, but worse. More pungent. It made my eyes water."

He blew out a breath. It was the same smell he'd encountered when he'd chased the creature in the swamp. A thought flashed through his mind and he leaned over to smell her clothing.

"What are you doing?" she asked, staring at him as if he'd lost his mind.

"If the smell was really the creature itself, some of the smell would be on your clothes, but I don't smell anything."

She lifted her arm and sniffed her blouse. "You're right, but that doesn't have to mean it was a fake."

"Then what is another explanation?"

"I don't know. Maybe it's his feet that smell or other body parts that I don't want to think about. Skunks have scent glands. Maybe he does, too."

"And this wild creature knew how to open a truck door?"

"Maybe."

The sheer ridiculousness of their conversation hit Tanner and he laughed. "You realize it's the middle of the night, you were attacked and we're actually discussing the possibility of scent glands and elevated thinking ability on a creature for which there is no proof that it even exists."

"I—"

She stopped speaking when Emmett Vernon rushed into the living room, a man with a medical bag close on his tail.

"You're awake?" Vernon said and glared at Tanner.

"Sorry," Tanner said, wondering if he was going to spend his entire night apologizing. "She just woke up. I was about to come tell you."

He rose from the couch and let the doctor inspect Josie.

"Can someone get me a warm, damp rag?" the doctor asked. "I want to remove the blood so I can get a better look at that gash."

"I'll do it," Vernon said, and headed for the kitchen.

The doctor turned Josie's head from side to side, studying the gash. "Do you know what hit you?"

"A rock, maybe? I think I blacked out for a bit and when I woke up, he was running with me. I screamed and he dropped me, then ran off into the swamp. My head must have struck something when I hit the ground."

Vernon hurried back into the living room with a wet dishrag and passed it to the doctor. He dabbed gently at the wound, lifting the blood from her forehead, then leaned in for a closer look.

"Could have been a rock," the doctor said. "It's a small gash. Won't need stiches, but being on the head, they bleed like crazy. Always looks worse than it is."

"What about her blacking out?" Tanner asked.

"Based on what she describes, I'd say the first time was out of fear. The second was most certainly because of the blow to the head."

"Concussion?" Tanner asked.

"Perhaps, but a light one, if any. I'll clean this up and butterfly the gash." He patted Josie's leg. "You'll be fine, young lady. Still, if it's all the same, I'd like to see you at my office tomorrow for an X-ray. Just to be safe."

"She'll be there," Tanner said, ignoring Vernon, who smirked.

The doctor nodded. "And I want you to take it easy for a couple of days. You will likely have a mild headache, but if it gets painful, or if you become weak or nauseated, then I want you to get to a hospital straightaway."

"Okay," Josie said.

Given her weak voice and complete lack of argument, Tanner knew Josie felt worse than she was willing to admit.

"Doc?" Tanner asked. "Is it okay for me to move her upstairs to her bedroom? She'll be more comfortable there and I can fetch anything she needs from the kitchen."

The doctor nodded. "Bed is definitely the best place for her, and she should stay in it awhile. I'm not sure what your role is here, Mr., er…"

"LeDoux," Tanner said, and extended his hand to the doctor. "Tanner LeDoux. Ms. Bettencourt hired me to look into the problems she was having with vandalism."

The doctor studied Tanner as he shook his hand. "Seems those problems just got worse."

Vernon snorted and Tanner frowned. "Yes, sir, but that's a situation I'm going to correct."

"It's not his fault," Josie said. "I knew if someone really had it in for me, they'd escalate if I hired someone to investigate. I just didn't expect a response this quickly. I'll be more prepared from now on."

The doctor didn't look particularly happy at her response, but he must have known her well enough not to argue. He looked back at Tanner. "I'm going to hold you to your promise, young man. Josie's father was one of my oldest friends. That makes her family."

Tanner nodded. "You have my word. I'll keep her safe."

Josie blew out a breath of exasperation. "Don't I get a say?"

"No." All three of the men spoke at once.

She looked from one determined face to another and finally sighed. "I give up. If there's nothing else you need to check, I'd like to go to bed now."

She pushed herself into an upright position. Three hands reached out to her, but she waved them all away, swung her legs around and rose from the couch. "You guys can fight over who's going to bring me aspirin and a soda. I'm going to take a long, hot bath and then climb into bed."

Tanner watched as she disappeared up the stairs. Then he turned back to the other men. "You have to admire her spunk," he said.

"She's as hardheaded as her dad," Vernon said, "and not as wise, which makes for a dangerous combination."

The doctor clapped Vernon on the shoulder. "She's young yet, and Franklin could be as big a fool as anyone if he decided to. The girl's got a good head on her shoulders. She'll be fine."

The doctor turned and pointed a finger at Tanner. "And if she's not, I'm paying you a visit."

"Yes, sir," Tanner said, and followed the doctor and Vernon to the door.

The doctor waved one hand over his shoulder and headed to his car.

"You didn't see anyone enter the house?" Tanner asked.

"No, and there wasn't anyone on the trail from my cabin. I couldn't sleep and figured after that stunt last night, I'm come check on the horses. I didn't see no light, either, but I'm not doubting your word on that."

"I should have been better prepared," Tanner said, mentally cursing himself.

Vernon shuffled a bit, then finally sighed.

"I assume you know how to use a weapon?" Vernon asked.

"Of course. Shotgun, rifle or pistol."

Vernon nodded. "Don't hesitate to use them. If anything happens to that girl, Franklin is going to come back and haunt me."

He pulled a cigarette from his pocket and walked out the door and across the lawn in the direction of his cabin. Tanner watched him walk away, wondering if he'd ever figure the man out. He was belligerent to Josie one minute, then worried about her the next.

So many things about Emmett Vernon simply didn't add up, but Tanner was going to keep crunching the numbers until they did.

Chapter Ten

Josie pulled on yoga pants and a T-shirt and towel-dried her damp hair. Her head still throbbed a bit, but her chest no longer ached. She supposed it had been anxiety that caused it to hurt in the first place, but she'd never felt anything like it in her life. Of course, she'd never been almost abducted from a creature out of a horror movie, either, so she supposed it was only right that she'd panicked.

She'd just walked back into her bedroom when there was a soft rapping at her door. "It's open," she called out as she picked up a comb and started working on her long tresses.

Tanner walked in, carrying a glass of soda and a bottle of aspirin. "The doctor said aspirin should be fine for tonight, but if they didn't work well enough, to let him know and he'll prescribe something stronger when you see him tomorrow."

"I'm sure the aspirin will be fine. My head doesn't hurt as much anymore."

Tanner nodded. "The adrenaline rush is over. Your blood flow and heart rate are back to normal. Not as much pressure on your head."

She put the comb back on her dresser and looked at him. "Sounds like you're speaking from experience."

"Lots of things happen when you're working in the swamp. I've been on the wrong end of trouble more than once, and I doubt it's the last time." He motioned to the bed. "Why don't you take a couple of aspirins and get some rest? That's the best thing for a head injury."

She propped the pillows up and climbed into bed, resting her back against the pillows. Tanner crossed the room and handed her the soda, then poured a couple of aspirins into her hand. As she swallowed the aspirin, he sat on the edge of her bed and stared down at the floor for a moment.

Finally, he looked back up and said, "I'm really sorry about this. It's all my fault. You hired me to protect you and your property, and I've only made things worse. I'm going to call my brothers first thing tomorrow and ask for one of them to take over your case."

"No, you're not!"

Tanner's eyebrows lifted at the strength of her reply, and instantly, she felt bad. She'd been thinking only of herself, not of him.

"I'm sorry," she said. "If you want to leave, I understand completely. You're a tracker, not a bodyguard. But if you're offering to leave because you think you somehow failed me, you're wrong."

"How can you say that? I was supposed to be tracking a vandal in the swamp. Instead, I started setting up a sting operation like I was a cop. I don't have the training for that, and it's something I never should have done. Look what happened."

"What happened is we made him nervous. He's reacting now. He'll make a mistake."

He raised one eyebrow. "That sounds like an interesting theory for a horse trainer."

"I watch a lot of *Law & Order.*"

He gave her a small smile and she could tell that some of the guilt had lifted off him.

"Look," she continued, "I knew the risks when I agreed to go into town with you tonight. And the reality is, it was going to happen now or later because I'm not going to quit. So whether he escalated tonight or two weeks from now, his response would have been the same. The difference is tonight I had you here to help."

He stared at her for so long that her body began to tingle. Suddenly, she realized how close he was to her, separated only by thin bedding and clothing. Even more disturbing was how much she wished there was even less between them.

He reached up and brushed a lock of her hair from her eyes. As his rough fingers stroked her soft skin, her body flashed with heat. Given that it was December, she was certain it wasn't the temperature in the room that had caused the response. He looked her directly in the eye for several seconds, and she would have sworn he was about to lean in and kiss her. Then he rose from the bed and went over to look out the window.

"I'll lock the door before I pull it shut." He picked up her cell phone from the dresser and handed it to her. "Keep this on your nightstand. If anything at all bothers you during the night, call me. If I don't answer, call the police."

"But—"

"No buts. I should never have left you waiting in the truck. I should have sent you back to town to get the sheriff. I'm not going to make the same mistakes again."

The stubborn look on his face was a dead giveaway that she would get nowhere arguing with him.

"Try to get some rest," he said before stepping out of the room and closing and locking the door behind him.

She stared at the closed door and sighed. Finally, she pulled her pistol out of her nightstand drawer and checked to ensure that it was loaded and ready to fire, then placed it on the nightstand next to her cell phone.

Soon, she would slide down under the covers and try to stop her whirling mind long enough to sleep. Somewhere in the house, Tanner was probably still blaming himself for everything. Truth be known, she understood how he could think that way from his perspective, but from her own, she knew there was no way she would have left him in the house alone. Not tonight and not any other.

The television remote was right there on her bed, but she didn't pick it up. Even the most fascinating of programs couldn't top what was happening in her own home. She rose from the bed and pulled the curtains aside, staring out into the darkness.

Someone or something was out there. Even in the cloak of darkness and separated by glass and curtains, she could feel the eyes upon her.

THE INTRUDER LURKED AT the edge of the black swamp, watching the house as the lamp in Josie's bedroom clicked off. Kidnapping hadn't been part of the plan, but she'd been a sitting duck. It was too much temptation to resist.

If tonight didn't put the fear of God into her, then the intruder would have to come up with another idea. A key to Josie's house jingled in a duffel bag as the intruder lifted it from the ground.

The night's events had accomplished two things.

JOSIE GROUSED AND DRAGGED her feet over breakfast and generally delayed more than any ten females he'd ever seen, but Tanner finally got her in his truck and on the way to the doctor.

"I don't need to see the doctor," she grumbled for at least the tenth time as he drove into town. "I don't even have a headache."

"I made a promise to the man. Do you want me to be branded a liar *and* a fool?"

She blew out a breath and slumped in her seat. He looked over at her and grinned.

"Have you always been this spoiled?" he asked.

She sat up straight and glared at him. "Spoiled? I'll have you know I work my butt off. I'm no pampered princess, regardless of what some might think."

"I didn't say anything about working hard."

"Then what are you insinuating?"

"That aside from Vernon, you're used to men doing what you say."

She frowned. "Nothing could be further from the truth. Look, I'm not trying to be ungrateful. I know all of you are worried about me and trying to do what you think is right. And I know I'm making that more difficult than it has to be."

"No argument so far. You want to tell me why that's the case?"

She shrugged. "I guess I got used to taking care of myself for one. I don't have time to be off work if I want to open the bed-and-breakfast on time. And since I'm self-employed, I don't have insurance. All that testing comes directly out of my pocket."

Tanner glanced over at her and took in her stiff posture and the way she nibbled at her bottom lip. He understood being independent—understood it with a vengeance—but he didn't understand the rest of her concerns. If it had been someone without the last name

Bettencourt, he might have, but Josie could write checks for additional workers and get everything done on time if it was that important to her, and the cost of an X-ray was negligible in the big scheme of things.

If her inheritance wasn't immediately liquid, he was sure the doctor would bill her and allow her to get money shifted. Certainly, the man wasn't going to hold her hostage in his office for cash payment. All he could assume was that whatever the real problem was, she wasn't ready to tell him about it. As much as that frustrated him, he really couldn't blame her. When it came right down to it, he was barely more than a stranger, and he was hired help, to top it off.

It occurred to him that where Josie Bettencourt was concerned, "hired help" seemed to be his destiny.

He held in a sigh as he parked in front of the doctor's office on Main Street.

"While you get checked out," he said, "I'm going to have a talk with the sheriff. I'm sure he'll want to talk to you as soon as you're done."

"Oh, I doubt that. He doesn't like to talk to anyone who thinks he should actually do his job."

"Well, then he's going to be mighty unhappy, and I don't care. Rest assured, he *will* do his job. I'm not giving him a choice."

Josie gave him a small smile. "If I didn't despise the man so much, it would probably make me happy to see you lean on him. Unfortunately, that requires looking at him, so my enthusiasm is not where it ought to be."

Tanner laughed. "Tell me how you really feel."

Now she smiled for real. "That was the 'light' version."

"I think I might enjoy this," he said, and climbed out of the truck.

Josie exited the truck and gave him a wave as she walked up the sidewalk to the doctor's office. "I'll come see the fallout as soon as I'm done here," she said, and walked inside.

Sufficiently warned, Tanner set his jaw and strode across the street to the sheriff's department, but before he could enter the building, a young woman stopped him on the sidewalk.

"Tanner, right?" she asked, then looked at the ground.

He took a good look at her, then remembered where he'd seen her before. "Good morning, Marquette."

She looked up and gave him a shy smile. "I hope you enjoyed your ribs last night."

He nodded. "The ribs were excellent, as was the service."

Her eyes widened and a dark red flush crept up her neck and onto her face. "That's a very nice thing for you to say."

Tanner instantly felt a bout of compassion for the young woman. He'd been that person before—shy, hiding in corners, afraid to draw attention to himself. He hadn't morphed into an extrovert, but he'd finally become comfortable in his own skin…usually…most of the time. Okay, maybe he had some work to do, but he was way better off than Marquette.

"I'm going to have some coffee at the cafe," Marquette said, staring at the sidewalk again, "If you want to join me."

"I appreciate the invitation, but I'm on my way to speak to the sheriff."

She looked up again. "Is everything all right?"

"We had some trouble at Ms. Bettencourt's house last night. I want the sheriff to look into it."

"Is Josie okay?"

"She's fine, but neither of us is interested in a repeat event."

Marquette nodded. "Well, she's lucky she's got you looking out for her." She gave him a wistful smile. "I guess I'll see you around."

"You have a nice day, and thanks again for the coffee offer."

"Anytime," she said, and started down the sidewalk toward the cafe.

Tanner took a deep breath and blew it out, mentally preparing himself for battle. Then he pushed open the door to the sheriff's department and walked inside.

An older woman with poofy brown hair sticking out in every direction called out a greeting to him from a copy machine in the corner of the reception area.

"Good morning, Ms...."

"Bartlett," the woman said as she ambled back to the desk with her copies, "but you can call me Cathy. What can I help you with this morning, Mr...."

"Tanner LeDoux."

"Ah, yes. You're the tracker that Josie hired. Heard about it this morning at the diner."

"I'd like to speak to the sheriff. Is he in?"

She leaned forward and whispered, "Doesn't move out of that chair unless it's time to eat."

"May I ask what this is about?" she asked in her regular voice.

Tanner held in a grin. "Yes, ma'am. There was an intruder out at the Bettencourt place last night, and he tried to drag Josie off into the swamp."

"Oh!" Cathy's eyes widened and she put her hand over her mouth. "Is Josie all right?"

"She hit her head on a rock and has a bit of a headache, but seems all right. She's at the doctor's office right now getting a thorough check."

Cathy nodded approvingly. "I know you young people don't think you need doctors unless you're missing a limb, but I'm glad she's getting checked. I lost my husband to a head injury."

Sympathy coursed through him. "I'm very sorry. How did it happen?"

"Got hit with a net frame working on his shrimp boat. Tossed back some aspirin and refused to see the doctor despite my nagging. Dropped dead three days later. He'd been bleeding in his brain."

"That's a sobering story, Cathy, and makes me happy that I insisted despite her protests."

She nodded and rose from her chair. "Follow me. The sheriff needs to find whoever attacked Josie. If it had happened before last night, you wouldn't have been there, and things could have gone very wrong. It's not safe, a young woman staying out in that big house. It's too remote."

"Emmett Vernon lives on property."

She waved a hand in dismissal. "Emmett's too busy gabbing at the general store or stalking through the swamp. Even if he was on property, he wouldn't hear anything happening at the main house all the way from his cabin. And you couldn't blast him out of there with dynamite, not even to protect Josie. The man's got issues."

"Yeah, I noticed the attitude."

"Got a lot of men with that problem in this town." She pointed her finger at the door with "Sheriff" stenciled on it. "Including this one," she whispered.

"Sheriff," she called out as she pushed open the door.

"There's a Tanner LeDoux here to see you about some problems at the Bettencourt place."

She stepped back and Tanner walked into the office, getting his first look of Bobby Reynard since they were teens.

He felt an unexpected amount of satisfaction when he saw that the bully who had embarrassed him in high school now had a beer belly and sagging biceps. Apparently, Cathy had been telling the truth—the man only moved to eat.

He stepped up to the desk and extended his hand, but Bobby didn't even bother to move forward and take it. Instead, he just stared at Tanner with a look that was part disgruntled, part bored.

Tanner sat in a chair in front of the desk, unwilling to be deterred by the man's rudeness. Apparently, not everyone matured after high school.

"If Josie sent you down here thinking you're going to get a different response than she did, you're wasting your time. Trouble with bears wasn't my job last week and it's still not. I hear you're some big-time tracker. You shouldn't have any problem with wildlife."

"I'm not here about bears. I'm here because someone attacked and tried to kidnap Josie in her driveway last night."

Bobby raised his eyebrows, clearly unperturbed. "I'm sure she was mistaken. Probably someone just wanted to talk to her, but being a frigid bitch, she assumed the worst."

Tanner clenched his hands by his side, exercising every ounce of control he had to keep himself from jumping out of the chair and pummeling the man into tomorrow. "The doctor came to see her last night. She's at his office right now getting tests run for a concussion. Does that sound like a pleasant conversation to you?"

"You don't say." Bobby sat up in his chair. "Did you see the guy who attacked her?"

"No. I saw a light in the upstairs window of her house when we pulled up the drive. I left her in the truck while I went inside to check it out. He grabbed her out of the truck."

"Did you find someone in the house?"

"No, but a window on the back of the house was unlocked, and I found tracks beneath the window in the flower bed this morning."

"Can Josie describe her attacker?"

Tanner hesitated. He'd been dreading this part of the conversation all morning. "Yes, but it's not going to do you much good. He was wearing a disguise."

"A mask or something?"

"No. An entire costume."

Bobby's jaw set in a hard line. "I know you're not about to tell me that she was attacked by the Honey Island Swamp Monster. Given your background, you of all people know better than to come into my office with that nonsense."

"Look, I don't think there's a real monster stalking Josie, but I do believe her description, and that means someone is going to very creative lengths to scare her."

Bobby sighed. "You seem like a nice guy just trying to do his job, so I'm going to give you some advice. Josie Bettencourt is not what she seems. On the surface, it's all mannered and nice and easy on the eyes, but below the surface is a desperate woman who will do anything to ensure that her bed-and-breakfast is successful. Now, just what do you think it would do for bookings if news gets out that the Honey Island Swamp Monster has been spotted on her property?"

Tanner frowned, not liking that niggling feeling he'd just gotten. "Why would she be desperate? Clearly, her family has money."

"At one time, the Bettencourts were darn near royalty in this town. But rumor has it that Josie's dad got taken by his financial adviser and was near bankrupt before he died. Some think losing the money is what did him in."

"*Rumor* has it. So what you're saying is that no one knows for sure and everyone's making a huge assumption?"

"Call it whatever you'd like, but old man Bettencourt's financial adviser is doing a dime in Angola for embezzling his clients' money, and Bettencourt testified at the hearing. Doesn't take a detective to put those facts together. Then when Josie rushed home and got this fool idea of opening a bed-and-breakfast in her family home, I knew the score."

Tanner stared at the man, all of the pieces falling into place. Josie's working to the point of exhaustion. Her worry over the New Year's opening. Her refusal to hire more contractors or pay higher rates.

Could Bobby possibly be right? Was all of this the master plan of a clever woman who was desperate to hold on to her family home?

Bobby leaned forward in his chair. "I see you understand my line of thinking."

"I can understand why you'd draw those conclusions, but there're a number of things that don't add up. I tracked the creature through the swamp yesterday— saw it with my own eyes. Why hire me if it's all a ruse?"

"Credibility? If a professional tracker says there's

something out in the swamp, then that makes it all the more compelling to investigate. You say you saw the creature?"

Tanner could hear the skepticism oozing from the man's voice, and couldn't really blame him. It was an outlandish sort of thing to buy into.

"Yes."

"'Bout how far away were you from this creature?"

Tanner immediately knew where he was going with his line of questioning. It was the same direction Tanner would have gone if the situation were reversed. He resented, a bit, being on the wrong side of the desk.

"About twenty yards away when I saw part of the head. It was easily over six feet tall. I gave chase for about a mile through the swamp, but the creature out-maneuvered me and lost me by jumping in the bayou. By the time I got around the bend, he was out of sight and the root system on the banks didn't allow for me to zero in on his exit point."

The sheriff nodded, looking a bit smug.

"I want to be clear," Tanner said. "I don't believe in monsters, but I know what I saw, and there is no way that was Josie in a suit. The size was all wrong."

"Oh, I agree that it couldn't have been Josie. But she could easily be paying someone to do the job. Makes more sense, really."

"If she paid someone to create this buzz, then why was she attacked?"

"You only got her word on that. She got away and wasn't seriously injured. If something that size really wanted to hurt her—man or creature—couldn't he have done a better job?"

Tanner clenched his jaw, trying to find a good argument to the sheriff's words, but unable to come up with one. The reality was, if everything he'd said about Josie's father was true, the sheriff's theory wasn't exactly that far-fetched. He didn't want to believe it, but couldn't stop that small feeling of doubt.

"I can see you're torn over this," the sheriff said. "I get that. She's a beautiful woman and you're trying to do your job. Tell you what—I'll drive out to the house and take a look around. If I come up with anything that indicates something different than what I suspect, I'll launch a full investigation. How's that sound?"

Tanner knew the man would do only the most cursory of checking up, but he also knew when he'd been outgunned. He nodded and rose from the chair.

"Thank you for your time," he said, and exited the building.

As soon as Josie was done at the doctor's office, they were going home for a long discussion. This time without the lies.

Chapter Eleven

Josie glanced over at Tanner, wondering again what he was thinking. He'd been waiting outside the doctor's office when she walked out and had asked about the checkup, but had only given her a cursory nod when she'd told him everything was fine.

She'd asked about his visit with the sheriff, but he'd only said he'd given Bobby the information and at this time, the sheriff didn't need to speak to her. She had no doubt about that. If Bobby had even taken a note during his conversation with Tanner, it had probably gone straight into the trash as soon as Tanner had left the sheriff's office.

He'd remained silent while driving back to her house, staring straight down the road, his expression one of concentration and aggravation. She could appreciate the sentiment. Bobby tended to leave her feeling aggravated, as well, and she supposed he was thinking about how to find her attacker. But his attitude was such a departure from the tenderness and care she'd seen the night before in her bedroom that she was a little confused.

As he pulled up in front of her house, he blew out a breath and looked over at her. "We need to talk."

"Okay…" His tone led her to believe she wasn't going to like the conversation.

"Are you broke?" he asked.

Her jaw involuntarily dropped open and she clamped it shut. Of all the questions in the world that she'd expected, that one hadn't even been on the list.

"I don't see what business that is of yours," she said, offended at the question and his tone.

"It's my business if you're staging this creature sighting to get business for your bed-and-breakfast."

A flush started up her neck and crept across onto her face and she struggled against the urge to slap him, because she knew that idea hadn't originated with Tanner. "If you believe that, then I guess your work here is done. Please have Alex send me an invoice."

She jumped out of the truck, slamming the door behind her, and ran into the house, holding back tears of shame and frustration. This was exactly the kind of situation she'd been trying to avoid. Even worse, it had been thrown in her face when she was completely unprepared and by the person she least expected to hear it from.

Itching for a drink, she hurried into the kitchen and opened the refrigerator, then changed her mind. Alcohol wasn't the answer. It never was. During her modeling career, she'd seen too many people ruin their lives with alcohol and drugs. She'd made it this long without using a crutch, and she wasn't about to start using one now.

Instead, she grabbed a Diet Coke, walked over to the picture window in the breakfast nook and stared out across the lawn. What in the world had she done to deserve all of this? Maybe she was making a huge mistake in fighting to keep her family home. Her family was all gone and aside from Adele, no one in Miel seemed to like her much. What was she sticking around for—a bunch of wood and grass that she couldn't even afford to maintain, much less pay for?

A single tear rolled down her cheek and she brushed it away with her fingers. At one time, she'd loved it here, had felt safe here. Now everything had changed. She'd come home hoping to start a new life with familiar, happy surroundings and now she didn't even feel safe in her own home. She'd felt completely and totally alone when she'd fled France and come back home, only to find that back home, she was totally alone, as well.

"I'm sorry," Tanner said, his voice soft.

She brushed another tear from her face and turned to look at him. "Sorry you were wrong, or sorry for assuming that horrid gossip about me was true?"

"Both, but I'm not going to take the entire blame for my question. Only for the way I presented it."

"So you still think I'm lying? That I'm the kind of person who could risk my own safety and drag other people into my plot just to get some free marketing?"

"I saw you last night, and I think your fear was real. So unless you're the best actress in the world, I don't think you planned the attack. But I do think you're lying. Even if only by omission, the truth is, you're not telling me everything I'm dealing with here."

She bristled at his words, knowing they were true, but unwilling to explain herself. "My personal business is none of your concern. You're supposed to track the vandal, not get involved in things that don't concern you."

"That's true enough, but when your personal business limits the amount of cooperation I get from law enforcement and even your own foreman, it becomes my concern. I can't do all of this alone. Even if I wanted to be in two places at once, I can't track the vandal while

protecting you, and you need protecting. That should
be clear after last night."

She turned back to the window and sucked in a
breath, blowing it slowly out. He was right, but that
didn't mean she had to like it. If she forced herself into
his point of view, she could understand his frustration.
She was setting him up for failure. No one man could
do everything she needed.

Perhaps in the beginning, she'd only needed a tracker
and could have kept her embarrassing secrets to herself,
but things had changed and now she had a decision to
make—either she told Tanner the truth and asked for
his help working through the mess she was in or she
called Sam and took his client up on their offer to buy
her property.

One of those options was only slightly less painful
than the other.

Stupid. You'd let pride ruin what you want?

Her dad's voice echoed in her mind. He'd been a
strong, prideful man himself, and stubborn as they
came, but he'd always told her that there came a time
in everyone's life when they had to ask for help. It would
likely be embarrassing and it made one feel like a failure, but the reality was, at some point in time, one person couldn't do it alone.

She'd thought she could never feel more mortified
than she had that day in France. That day that her entire world had come unraveled, but standing here in her
kitchen, she didn't even know how to start the conversation with Tanner without dissolving into tears.

He placed his hand on her shoulder and lightly
squeezed. "I want to help, but you've got to trust me."

His words were that last chink in the brick, and the
entire dam burst. Tears flowed freely from her eyes as

she sobbed. Tanner stepped in front of her and wrapped his arms around her, drawing her close to him. She circled his strong body with her arms and pressed her face against his chest, unable to stop the flood of emotion.

She had no idea how long they stood that way, but finally, the last tear had fallen and relief washed over her. Sniffing, she pushed back from his chest and realized his shirt was damp with her tears.

"I've ruined your shirt," she said, unable to meet his eyes.

"It's nothing that a washing won't fix," he said softly. Then with one finger, he lifted her chin up so that their eyes met. "I didn't mean to upset you like this."

She shook her head. "It's not you. Your words were just the final straw in years of pushing things to the back of my mind instead of facing them. It was going to happen eventually. I'm just sorry you caught the raw end of it."

"Do you want to talk about it?"

"Yes and no. I think I need to talk about everything, but at the same time, I'm horribly embarrassed about a lot of things, feel like a failure over others and…"

She stared down at the floor for a moment, then blew out a breath and looked back up at him. "I have a problem with trust. There's only one person left in this world who I trust right now."

"Adele?"

Josie nodded. "It's not personal. It's just that everyone else I've known aside from Adele and my parents have disappointed me. The fact that I believed in people wholeheartedly and found my judgment so sadly lacking forced me to retreat into trusting no one."

"I understand."

"Everyone says that, but do they really understand?"

"I think I do. Remember what I told you about my parents? Clearly, my dad wasn't trustworthy and beyond that, he was a horrible father. Always making promises that he never kept. That's hard on kids."

"But you had your mother."

"My mother drank herself to death, pining over a man she couldn't have all to herself. She never bothered to raise me. She barely noticed me."

The hurt and anger were so clear in his voice that Josie hurt for him—the little boy inside whose childhood had been robbed by two selfish adults. Immediately, she felt guilty for her accusation. Tanner had a lot more reasons not to trust people than she did. At least she'd had two loving, caring parents who thought the sun set on her.

"Now I'm the one who needs to apologize," she said. "You've had worse reasons than me to stop trusting people."

"Perhaps, but if we're going to figure all this out, we're going to have to trust each other, no matter what our better judgment tells us to do."

Josie nodded and reached out to clasp his hand. "I'm going to trust you with the truth, despite the fact that it's messy and embarrassing. No more secrets."

"No more secrets," he agreed and gave her hand a squeeze before releasing it and motioning to a chair at the breakfast table.

She slid into the chair and he took a seat directly next to her, turning his chair so that he was facing her.

She took a deep breath. "Bobby was telling the truth."

Tanner's eyes widened and she rushed to correct herself. "Not about faking the monster to get free advertising. I would never do something dishonest, no matter how bad things were. But he was right about my being broke."

"Do you want to talk about it?"

"Not really. It's in the past and nothing's going to change it. The short version is that my dad trusted the wrong man with his money. That man is currently in prison, but the money he stole from clients is nowhere to be found."

He frowned. "I'm sorry. It takes a special kind of evil to steal people's life savings. I hope he gets what he deserves behind bars."

"So do I."

"I thought modeling paid big money. I mean, I see framed pictures all over the house of you in ads."

"It paid well, that's true. Unfortunately, I'd sent a lot of the money home to my dad to invest for me. I knew about the trial, of course, but I didn't find out just how much we'd lost until after my dad died. I guess he couldn't bring himself to tell me."

"You didn't find out before you bought the horses," he concluded.

"No, or I wouldn't have done it, but my dad's investor isn't the only place I lost money. I invested a good amount in a man I thought loved me, a photographer. Turns out he was more interested in the financial backing and connections I could get him. Once his career took off, he pursued sleeping with my friends as diligently as he had his career."

"They weren't your friends," Tanner said quietly.

"You're right, of course. But I was young and foolish and not in the least bit ready for the brutality of the fashion world."

"How long were you with him?"

"Three years. We'd celebrated our dating anniversary one night with a romantic dinner. He'd begged off the after-dinner fun claiming he didn't feel well. Being the dutiful girlfriend, I tucked him in and tended to him until I had to go to work the next morning. I was halfway to the work site when I realized I'd forgotten a pair of shoes I was supposed to wear for the shoot."

She stopped for a minute, that day playing through her mind as vividly as if it were happening right now. No matter how much time elapsed, she could still see it all so clearly. Her quietly unlocking the apartment door, hoping to slip in and get her shoes without waking him from his sleep.

Instead, she'd interrupted her boyfriend and the woman she'd thought was her closest friend in the middle of their bedroom activities.

"You walked in on him," Tanner said.

"Yes. And the woman I thought was my best friend. It had been going on for months, and I was horrified to find that I was the only one who didn't know."

Tanner slid forward in his chair, until his face was only inches from hers. He ran one finger down her cheek as his eyes locked on hers. "He was a fool."

Josie's breath caught in her throat as he leaned in. He was going to kiss her and at the moment, she couldn't think of a single thing she wanted more.

His lips brushed softly against hers, and she closed her eyes, relishing every second. He deepened the kiss, parting her lips with his own. Every inch of her skin began to tingle as her tongue mingled with his…softly, tenderly.

"Josie!" Emmett Vernon's voice boomed from the front of the house.

Tanner jumped up from the chair and went to stand by the window, his back to her. Josie sighed and called out to let Vernon know she was in the kitchen. It figured the foreman would finally get industrious about his job at the worst possible time.

The foreman's heavy footsteps echoed down the hall, and a couple of seconds later, he entered the kitchen. Immediately, he gave her a once-over.

"What did the doctor say?"

"He said I'm fine."

"Uh-huh. That's it?"

"No, he said to take it easy for a couple of days."

Vernon frowned. "Which you have no intention of doing, of course."

"She'll take it easy," Tanner said, and turned from the window. "At least for a day."

"You going to stick around here and make her?" Vernon asked, the skepticism clear in his voice.

"That's exactly what I'm going to do."

Josie shook her head. "I don't need a babysitter. I'll be fine here alone. You two gentlemen can just go about your business."

Vernon narrowed his eyes at Tanner. "Shouldn't you be trying to track her attacker?"

"I was out before sunrise. It didn't take me long to discover everything there was to find."

"Which is what, exactly?"

"That the tracks led in a big loop that came out of the swamp right on the back lawn near the barn."

Vernon narrowed his eyes at Tanner as Josie sucked in a breath. "Why didn't you tell me?" she asked.

"Because I was more concerned about your health, so I was going to wait until we knew you were in the clear. There's nothing you could have done about it this morning any more than you can now."

"You're sure about the tracks?" Vernon asked.

Tanner nodded.

"But why would someone do that?" Josie asked.

"Because he wouldn't leave tracks across the pasture," Vernon said. "And from here, he can easily access three roads in a half-mile stretch. He probably had a vehicle parked somewhere."

Josie looked at Tanner for confirmation.

"He's right," Tanner said.

"So it's a dead end?" Josie asked. "There's nothing you can do?"

"Not about that particular incident."

Vernon shook his head. "Well, she's not paying you to sit around in the house playing nursemaid."

Tanner looked Vernon straight in the eye, his posture rigid. "Who says I'm on the clock today?"

Vernon studied him for several seconds and Josie could practically feel the testosterone moving through the air. Finally, he gave Tanner a single nod and turned back to Josie. "I've got the crew working on the southeast fences today. If you need anything, send Tanner to get me."

Josie watched Vernon walked down the hall and waited until she heard the front door close before turning back to Tanner.

"You're not telling me something. We said no secrets."

"I know, but I could hardly tell you that Vernon could have been your attacker while the man was standing in your kitchen."

Josie sucked in a breath. "No, he couldn't…he wouldn't…"

"Perhaps, but when I ran out of the swamp with you, Vernon was leaning against your barn smoking a cigarette. He claims he couldn't sleep and came to check on the horses, but it would have been the easiest thing in the world for him to stash the suit in the swamp, then calmly stroll across the pasture and light one up."

Josie's mind raced with the possibilities, but she couldn't think of a single thing to say that would prove Tanner was wrong. As much as she didn't want to believe it, Emmett was in the right place at the right time to have been her attacker.

"But what would he have to gain?" she asked.

"You'd have to tell me that. The man was your father's employee for a long time. Did your dad leave him anything in his will?"

"Yes, he left him ten percent of the business. There wasn't really anything else and the ranch was already in trouble, so even that was more of an albatross than an inheritance."

"Was the property part of the business?"

"Yes."

"So if you sold it, he'd get ten percent of the proceeds."

"Yes, but once the bank takes their share, the sale would net maybe five hundred thousand. His cut would only be fifty thousand and he'd have to pay capital gains tax on that. Hardly worth going to jail for."

"Maybe, but people have gone to jail for a lot less."

"I—" She blew out a breath. "I know you're right, but I just can't believe Emmett would do something like that."

"There's something else." He told her about the conversation he'd overheard between Vernon and the store owner the night before.

"I'm sorry I didn't tell you sooner," he said, "but things got a little crazy. Do you have any idea what they're up to?"

"Not with any certainty. I know Emmett's always talked about hunting alligator during season. All landowners get tags, but we've always sold them to professionals for the hunting. Depending on the price for the gators, it can pay very well if you can land the big ones. Emmett knows every inch of these bayous. He'd know where to find the big gators."

"Alligator season is in June. Would he be planning something for it now?"

"I don't know." She shook her head. "The longer this goes on, the more I think I don't know anything at all, and that what I thought I knew is all wrong. I want to believe Emmett and Ted are just plotting an alligator hunt or starting a fishing tour business or something else equally as innocuous, but I understand that you have to investigate every avenue."

He nodded.

"This would be so much easier if it turned out to be someone nasty, like Mack Prevet, but I guess he's out of the running since there's no way he left the bar and got to the house before we did."

"I wouldn't say that."

"What do you mean?"

"Mack disappeared about an hour before we left the bar. Plenty of time to get to your house and gain access. And as we were sitting in his bar, he knew the house was empty."

Josie stared. "I didn't even notice." Mentally, she chided herself for being so lost in having a good time with Tanner that she hadn't even kept an eye on one of their suspects. Apparently, Tanner hadn't run into trouble staying focused, which was encouraging on a professional front but somewhat disappointing on a personal one.

"Clearly, you're better suited to this than I am. I promise to keep an open mind and stay out of your way."

"I appreciate that." He grabbed his pistol from the counter and slid it into his waistband. "I want to take a walk around the perimeter of the house to check for any weak points. Lock the doors behind me and keep your cell phone handy."

Josie nodded.

"Hey," Tanner said as he opened the back door. "If it makes any difference, I hope it's not Vernon."

As he shut the door behind him, Josie couldn't help hoping so, as well.

Chapter Twelve

Tanner walked out of the shower and threw on jeans, T-shirt and tennis shoes, then hurried downstairs to the kitchen, where he'd left Josie "resting" twenty minutes before. She'd gone into a frenzy when he'd told her that his brothers were paying him a visit that afternoon. Neither he nor Josie had mentioned their earlier kiss, and after taking a cold shower, Tanner decided that was probably the best way to leave things. The last thing he needed in his life was another complication, and Josie Bettencourt was definitely not a simple woman.

He surveyed the kitchen, marveling at how quickly she'd accumulated such a mess. Mixing bowls were stacked on the kitchen island alongside canisters and plastic containers. A heavenly smell wafted from the oven.

"I brewed a fresh pitcher of tea because it's so warm," Josie said, "but if you would rather have coffee, I can start a pot. It will only take a few minutes."

"It's just my brothers, not royalty. You don't have to go to any trouble, especially when you're supposed to be resting."

She rolled her eyes. "Compared to a regular day, this is practically sedate. I can't lie around in bed all day. I'm just not made that way."

Tanner grabbed a soda from the refrigerator and sat down on a stool in front of the island.

Josie used a kitchen towel to wipe flour off her hands, then looked across the island at him. "Do you think they're going to take you off the case?"

Tanner paused a bit to consider her words. Certainly, Holt had been unhappy when Tanner had called him earlier to explain the bad turn of events that the case had taken, but he didn't think his brother's request for the three of them to meet had been precipitated by his phone call.

"I don't think so," Tanner said. "I got the impression that there's something else going on that they want to discuss with me."

"But wouldn't it have been easier for you to go back to Vodoun since both of them are there?"

"I refused to leave you here alone, and Holt agreed. Besides, it's the same distance from Vodoun to Miel as it is from Miel to Vodoun, and they're riding together," he joked.

She visibly relaxed a bit, then frowned. "I hope it's nothing serious. What am I saying? They're driving out to the middle of nowhere to talk to you. Of course it's serious."

She bit her lower lip. "Do you have any idea what it is?"

"None whatsoever," Tanner replied, and that was the truth. He didn't have any earthly idea why Holt's voice sounded strained or why he'd insisted on talking to him today, but he knew with certainty that he wasn't going to like it.

The crunch of gravel disrupted his thoughts and he rose from the chair as Josie grabbed a potholder.

"That must be them," she said, rushing to the oven.

"And I don't have everything ready. Can you please let them in? Heavens, I have got to do some serious work on my hostess skills."

Tanner smiled at her unnecessary panic as he strolled outside to greet Holt and Max as they stepped out of Holt's Jeep. Max looked up at the house and the surrounding grounds and whistled.

"Pretty fancy digs," Max said. "No wonder you didn't want to leave. This beats the hell out of your apartment."

Tanner grinned and shook his brother's hand. "I don't own the television remote, so there's a trade-off."

Holt laughed. "I bet it's even been cleaned this century, though."

Tanner let go of Max's hand and reached out for his big brother's. Max and Holt were only months apart in age, but Holt had always been the brother Tanner looked up to. He had always been the strongest, fastest, smartest of all the kids and he hadn't missed a step as an adult. Tanner wished he could latch onto his brother's secret. Max's, too, for that matter, as both his brothers seemed infinitely fulfilled with their lives.

Tanner released Holt's hand and gestured to the house. "Let's move inside. Josie's been in a whirlwind in the kitchen ever since I told her you were coming. She's got something that smells like heaven in the oven. I'm hoping it's ready for public consumption."

"I hope she didn't go to any trouble," Max said.

"Cooking is always trouble," Holt said.

"Only when Alex is doing it," Max teased.

Tanner laughed. Holt's wife, Alex, was beautiful and smart and tough, but she completely fell apart on the domestic side of things. Holt did most of the cooking at their house. Tanner suspected it was in self-defense.

"Asking Josie not to play hostess in her own home would be like asking me to stop breathing. I get the impression her mother was big on that kind of thing." Tanner's mind flashed back to the many mornings he'd spent setting up tables and chairs on the back lawn so that Josie's mother could host whatever group she'd gotten involved with. Audrey Bettencourt had been every definition of a lady—educated, beautiful, refined, kind and passionate about helping others in the community. Tanner had thought she was the most fantastic woman he'd ever met, next to Holt's mother.

If only Josie's father hadn't placed his trust in the wrong man, Josie could be holding court at the estate the way her mother had—worrying about helping others get by instead of desperately trying to hold on to the only home she'd ever known.

As they walked through the front door, Josie hurried down the hall to greet them. Tanner introduced her to his brothers, and she shook their hands, an anxious smile on her face.

"I've set you up in my father's study," she said as she motioned them across the living room to a set of open double doors off the side of the room. "I thought it would be more comfortable and private. I hope that's okay."

They walked into the room and looked around. Floor-to-ceiling bookcases covered every wall except the one that faced the front lawn. Every square inch of that wall contained windows with a sheer curtain that allowed sunlight to stream into the room.

A giant scrolled desk sat toward the back of the room, and directly in front of it were four black leather chairs forming a square and a coffee table in the middle of them, resting atop a bearskin rug. Glasses with ice, a pitcher of tea and a plate of chocolate chip cookies sat in the center of the coffee table.

Holt scanned the room in obvious appreciation. "If you don't mind, Josie. I'm going to take some pictures of this room before I leave. This is officially what I want my home office to look like."

Josie smiled. "My dad loved this room. He would have been pleased to know someone liked it so much they wanted to replicate it. I'll leave you gentlemen to it. Please let me know if you need anything else."

She stepped out of the study and pulled the massive carved wood doors closed behind her. Tanner poured tea and handed a glass to each of his brothers and they all sat in the chairs. Max reached for a cookie and gave a small sigh at the first bite.

"Homemade," Max said, and looked over at Tanner. "You might want to keep her."

Tanner shook his head. "Keeping her would imply that I have her in the first place."

Holt swallowed a huge bite of cookie and pointed his finger at Tanner. "You might want to try. Seriously. If I didn't love Alex, I'd go after Josie for her baking skills alone. Not that I failed to notice how easy on the eyes she is, mind you." He grinned at Tanner.

"She was a model," Tanner said, trying to play it off. "Of course she's beautiful. In case you two haven't noticed, the world is full of beautiful women, none of whom I've taken up with."

Holt looked over at Max and raised his eyebrows. Max stuffed an entire cookie in his mouth and nodded.

"He doth protest too much," Holt said to Max.

Tanner knew they were joking with him, probably trying to work themselves up to the real reason they were here. But talking about how attractive and wonderful Josie was hit a little too close to home for him to be able to make light of it. And the absolute last thing in the world he wanted to do was talk to his brothers about his warring emotions.

"I'm guessing the two of you didn't come all this way to discuss my personal life."

They both sobered and Holt shook his head. "Not your dating life, but what we need to discuss is personal. It's about our father."

Tanner frowned. In the hours between Holt's phone call and their arrival, his mind had come up with things that were important enough to precipitate an impromptu visit, but the only thing dire enough that he'd thought of was an illness—perhaps one of his brothers or their wives. And while he was relieved that none of them seemed to be the reason, he couldn't imagine what they had learned about their long-dead father that would send them here today.

"I don't know how much you remember about that day," Holt began.

"It's burned into my memory," Tanner said. "I know I was younger than you two, but it's not something you forget."

"I understand," Holt said. "Then you remember we were all going to play hooky at my house and had a bike race home from school. I got there first and saw a man leaving the house."

Tanner nodded. "You told the police, but they never really thought much about it."

"Yeah, and I let it go because I didn't have a choice. After I got back from my tour in Iraq and was appointed temporary sheriff of Vodoun, I combed all the original files on our father's murder, but there was nothing to go on. Until Alex's niece was kidnapped."

Tanner frowned. "I don't understand."

"The man who kidnapped her niece had a tattoo like the man I saw leaving the house. I'd never seen the tattoo before that day, and until Alex's niece was kidnapped, I'd never seen it again. But it turned up on two men—both criminals, both with no verifiable past and both dead, so no hope of questioning them."

"But we had a starting point," Max said. "A trail to follow, even if it was chilly and narrow. When I took my first case for the agency, I ran across the same tattoo. On another dead man with prints that didn't match anyone in the database."

"But this time," Holt continued, "our luck was a little better. He had a pin in his leg from an old break and we were able to trace it back to the real person. He was ex-military. Special Forces. He went AWOL ten years ago. Just based on observation and experience, I'd say the man who kidnapped Alex's niece was also ex-military."

Tanner stared at Holt, his mind trying to process everything his brother had laid out. Never in a million years had he imagined they'd have such a conversation. He'd always figured their father's murder was just one of the many that would go unsolved. He never thought that he and his brothers might make ground on the investigation over twenty years later.

"After all these years," Tanner said, "what are the odds that something like this crops up—making a connection to a case that's been dead for over two decades?"

Max nodded. "It's surreal. That's the way it felt to me, anyway, when Holt first told me."

"This tattoo," Tanner said. "What does it look like?"

Holt pulled a picture out of his pocket. "This is a pic of the tattoo on the guy from Max's case, but they're all the same."

Tanner took the picture from Holt and stared at the eye design of the tattoo. His pulse increased, and he felt his heart pounding in his chest.

"I've seen this tattoo before," he said.

His brothers' eyes widened and they straightened up in their chairs.

"Where?" Holt asked.

"On a guy I helped the DEA bust. He was running drugs through the Atchafalaya Basin. He looked suspicious to me—not like the regular hunters and fisherman—so I started poking around. Turns out he was running a couple mil a month of heroin up from Mexico."

Holt jumped up from his chair. "You helped bust him...so he's still alive?"

"Last I heard, he was doing twenty in Angola."

Max pulled out his cell phone. "I'll call my buddy at the NOLA Police Department and have him check. What's the guy's name?"

"Sebastian Portico."

While Max chatted with his cop buddy, Holt sat down again and Tanner looked over at him, taking in the expectant but also worried expression on his brother's face.

"You think our father was involved in something bad, don't you?" Tanner asked.

Holt sighed. "It's hard not to. All these guys have no past to speak of, we know their fingerprints have been altered and now we know for sure at least one of them was Special Forces. I'd bet he's not the only one."

"Mercenaries?"

"Maybe. All I know for certain is it's organized and deadly."

"Our father wasn't in the military."

"No, but he had a lot of business and a lot of money." Holt looked directly at Tanner, his expression grim. "What if he didn't make it all legally? What if we inherited blood money?"

Tanner frowned. He didn't like the thought, either.

"That's not on us," Tanner said. "We weren't even involved with him as a father, much less in his business. You're doing a good thing with your inheritance— starting the agency and taking on cases from people who don't have other options. Don't let yet another bad decision in the ten million bad decisions he made keep you from doing what's right now."

Holt gave him a small smile. "How did you get so smart?"

"I had an older brother who knocked it into me."

Max hung up the phone. "He's going to make sure Portico hasn't been transferred and see what's required to get us an interview."

"I wouldn't put too much faith in Portico being helpful," Tanner warned. "He clammed up during trial and refused to talk at all, even in his own defense."

Holt nodded. "Assuming he's part of something bigger, that's to be expected. Maybe we can talk to the prosecutor and tell him what we've got. See if he can put some pressure on Portico from his end."

Max slid back into his seat and grabbed a couple of cookies. "Well, since we're finished with old business, let's get back to new business. How's the investigation going, Tanner?"

Tanner shook his head. "I'm worried that I'm not cut out for this."

"Why do you say that?" Holt asked.

Tanner told them about the sightings of the creature,

the attack on Josie, Vernon's suspicious behavior and Josie's precarious financial position.

"It seems there's a whole lot of things going on," Tanner finished, "but none of them make sense. It's a bunch of moving pieces that don't form a clear picture."

Max nodded. "Police work was always like that. The hardest part about an investigation was sorting through all the crap to figure out what was relevant to the case. It was never clear-cut like they show on television."

"Max is right," Holt agreed. "You're not experiencing anything outside the norm. I know it feels out of sorts. I felt the same way when I started investigating. The military was straightforward for me, like tracking was for you. Once you have to involve yourself personally with people, things get complicated fast."

"It's not just that…" Tanner paused, not having any idea how to say what he needed to say.

"It's the swamp," Max said quietly. "Things don't feel right there."

Tanner let out a breath of relief. "Yes. How did you… Do you…"

"We both feel it," Holt said. "The swamps in Mystere Parish aren't like anywhere else. Things happen here that can't be explained."

"When I was a kid," Tanner said, "my mom always yelled at me for being fanciful. As I got older, I concocted all kinds of elaborate reasons for the things I saw. When I left, I convinced myself I'd imagined everything, but all the same, I never wanted to come back. That's why I went to Baton Rouge to work. That and other reasons."

"Are you having second thoughts about returning?" Holt asked.

Tanner nodded. "And thirds and fourths and one hundred eighty seconds."

"We get it," Max said. "I promise I'm not being glib. Both of us have had…experiences, let's say, that were outside what we'd call normal."

"When you were boys, maybe—" Tanner started.

"No," Holt interrupted. "He means recently. We don't talk about it much because people who haven't experienced it tend to look strangely at you, but I promise you, there's nothing you can tell us about the Mystere Parish swamps that we won't believe, Alex and Colette, as well."

Tanner felt as if a huge weight had been lifted from his shoulders. If these men and their wives also thought things were amiss in the swamps, then he no longer doubted his instincts. He began to recount what had happened the day he'd seen the creature.

Holt nodded. "We never doubted Josie's description of what she'd seen. The biggest part of what Alex does is assess potential clients for sanity and truth-telling and she thinks Josie is as sane as you and I."

"I never doubted her, either," Tanner said, "but I've been operating under the assumption that someone was trying to scare her."

"Wearing a suit, you mean?" Max asked.

"Exactly."

"It's a sound idea," Holt said. "What's got you questioning yourself now?"

Tanner stood and paced over to the window to stare outside. Finally, he ran one hand through his hair and turned back to face his brothers. "It was tall—almost seven feet—and there was nothing it could have been standing on. I checked. It moved incredibly fast, and there is no way a man could have stayed underwater the length of the bayou without oxygen."

"I suppose some of the height could be built into the suit," Max suggested. "You know, like he's really looking out of the mouth so that it appears taller than it is."

Holt nodded. "That's a good thought."

"Maybe. I don't know." Tanner stepped back to his chair and sat down, staring at the rug.

"The swamp went silent right before I saw him," Tanner said. "You know, how it does when a big predator is close by? Except even the insects were quiet. I've hunted killer bear and gators and all manner of wildcats, but I've never experienced something like that. Like the whole swamp was holding its breath."

He looked up at his brothers, still half expecting them to be looking at him as if he were crazy, but instead, they both wore serious expressions.

"I don't have an answer for you," Holt said, "but I can tell you to trust your instincts. If things feel off, then they probably are. You know the swamps better than any of us. If you say something's not right, then it's not. It's that simple."

Max nodded.

Tanner looked back and forth between them. "You're telling me that you actually think there's a chance that a real monster lives in the Honey Island Swamp?"

Holt shrugged. "Things that none of us can explain exist all over this world. Why not a swamp monster?"

Tanner laughed. "I don't know whether to be relieved that you don't think I'm crazy or worried that all of us are."

"Oh, well," Max said, "it goes without saying that we're all crazy. But that doesn't mean we're wrong."

Holt rose from the chair and clapped Tanner on the

shoulder. "You're doing a fine job here. If you need anything, give me a call. I need to get back for an evening appointment."

Max rose, as well, palming a few more cookies on his way out of the chair. "I'll let you know as soon as I hear about Portico."

"Thanks," Tanner said, his mind flashing back to the reason for his brothers' visit.

He walked them to the front door and lifted a hand to wave as they drove away, still trying to come to grips with the fact that his father's murder might be solved over twenty years later...and by his own sons.

ALEX CHAMBERLAIN HANDED her husband a bottle of beer and slid down next to him on their living room couch. Holt grabbed the beer with one hand and slung his other arm around his wife.

"Can you believe this is the first chance we've had to talk since lunch?" she asked. "How did it go with Tanner today?"

"Great, actually," Holt said, and filled Alex in on the information Tanner had provided. "It might come to nothing, but at least it's another lead to pursue."

"And how did Tanner take everything?"

Holt smiled at his psychiatrist wife. "Always the therapist, huh?"

"Tanner's family. I tend to care about family."

"I know. He seemed to take it all well. He was surprised, of course, but that's hardly unexpected."

"But?"

He shook his head. "There's no getting anything past you, is there?"

Alex grinned. "No, and I don't know why you even bother to try."

"Tanner didn't say anything that makes me think he's having trouble with the situation, but I get the impression he's working through some things."

"Like Max was when he returned home?"

"Maybe." Holt sighed. "Our father really screwed us up, didn't he? At least I had Mom, who did everything she could to make up for my father's shortcomings. Max's mother was a far second to my mother, but Tanner's mother made her look like a prize."

"She was an alcoholic, right?"

"Yeah, I think so. I didn't realize it when we were kids, but looking back as an adult, you see things for what they were. I think some of her boyfriends hit Tanner, too."

"Oh, no!" The heartbreak in Alex's expression was clear.

"He never would say, even when I asked, but no one's that clumsy. Not even a child."

Alex shook her head. "Make sure Tanner knows you're there for him. If he's still got unresolved issues over his childhood, he's eventually going to need to talk to someone. Otherwise, they'll continue to eat at him."

"I know. But you can't make a man talk to you, especially about emotional things. He knows I'm here. That's a step in the right direction."

Alex leaned over to kiss him. "You know I love you, right?"

"I love you, too."

"So, are you even going to ask me why I was late tonight?"

Holt took one glance at the excited expression on Alex's face and knew she was bursting to tell him something important.

"I'll bite," he said. "Why were you late?"

"I found the son of that attorney we were looking for in France."

Holt straightened. "What about the attorney?"

"Died years ago, but the son was more than happy to talk to me about the case."

"That's surprising. You told him you think his dad helped broker the sale of kidnapped girls and he was happy to talk about it?"

"Apparently, his father spent the last decade of his life in prison for embezzling clients' funds, so the son wasn't interested in protecting his father's reputation."

"I guess that's something to be thankful for. Was he able to tell you anything?"

"Yep. Because of the trial, all his father's records had been audited. He said there were three adoptions recorded for that year. He's going to get me the original files so that we can track down the families that bought the girls."

Holt blew out a breath. The three elementary-aged girls had disappeared from Vodoun over thirty years ago. When Alex's niece disappeared a couple of months ago, Holt and Alex had searched for her niece and in finding her, had discovered the fate of the girls who had disappeared over three decades before.

One of the promises they had made when they opened their detective agency was to try and find those girls, even though they'd be in their thirties today.

"You know," Alex said, "the odds of them having been treated well are low. They were all six or older. Most likely they were acquired as domestic help."

"You mean slaves."

Alex sighed. "Yeah."

"So, assuming we find them and they want to come

home, they'll need someone to talk to. I bet you've got that covered."

"You know I'd do anything…. When I think about what happened to them and what their parents have gone through all these years not knowing, it's just heartbreaking."

Holt nodded. "I know it can't fix things, but there's money to be had in it. A civil suit against the estate might pave the way for them to start new lives in the U.S., if that's something they're interest in doing."

"Sounds like you've got it all figured out." Alex smiled. "I married such a smart man."

"If only I could fix my own family."

Alex placed her hand on Holt's leg and gave it a squeeze. "Give Tanner some time. I know it's hard for you to see him struggling and not jump in, but he's a grown man. He won't appreciate your butting in. You sorted it all out and so did Max. Tanner was always the more serious of you three. Likely, he needs to contemplate things a little longer than you."

Holt squeezed his wife's shoulders and took another sip of his beer. If anyone had told him a year ago that he'd be settled in his hometown, married to Alex, he would have called them crazy. But now he couldn't imagine another life.

That same peace and sense of belonging was all he wanted for his little brother, because he knew it was something Tanner had never had before. More than ever, he hoped his wife was right.

Chapter Thirteen

Josie stood in the kitchen watching Tanner check his pistol, hands on her hips and trying to control her frustration. Tanner had been quieter than usual after his brothers had left. She wondered why but wasn't about to ask.

"Why do you have to do the stakeout outside?" she asked. "Why can't you watch from one of the upstairs windows?"

"Because the grounds are too dark. The storage shed near the barn provides the best view of the house and the barn. If someone approaches from the swamp, I'll be able to see them."

"What if what you see isn't a man?"

"Doesn't matter. If I see someone trespassing on your property, I'm taking them down—man or beast."

"But it's not safe out there in the dark." Josie regretted the words as soon as they left her mouth. She knew it sounded foolish, but her attack was still too fresh in her mind for her to relax about Tanner lurking around outside in the middle of the night.

He stepped up to her and placed his hand on her arm. "This is nothing like last night."

"Are you reading my mind?" she grumbled.

"After what happened last night, it's not hard to

imagine what you're thinking. But this is different. This time, I'll be ready for him. Ready and waiting."

"I know it all makes sense logically, but I still don't want you to do it."

"It's my job," he said quietly. "I can't sit in this house waiting for things to come to me. That's putting you at bigger risk than preventing them from ever entering the house."

She blew out a breath. "I'm not going to win this argument, am I?"

"Did you ever really think you would?"

"Fine, then I'm coming with you."

He shook his head. "Absolutely not. You're going to stay inside and rest, just like the doctor said."

Josie held in the urge to scream. If she "rested" one minute longer, she was going to go stir-crazy. "So although you won't have any view at all of the front or sides of the house, you think I'm safer inside, even though he's already gotten in once."

"All the windows are closed and locked. I did a thorough check earlier."

"Sure, but what if the intruder stole keys last night? I have a whole drawer of them here in the kitchen. My dad kept more spares than a boat can haul—why, I have no idea—and it's not like he went to great lengths to hide them."

She pulled open a drawer in the kitchen island and pulled out an envelope clearly labeled "house keys." She dumped the envelope on the counter, and six keys came tumbling out.

Tanner stared at the keys in dismay. "How many were there before?"

"I have no idea. I never counted them."

"And you neglected to tell me this when the hardware store was still open and I could have changed the locks."

"I forgot, okay? Until you started making plans to sit in a toolshed all night and I realized I'd be alone in the house, I didn't think about the keys. It's not something I ever had to worry about before. This was a safe place…."

She already felt stupid enough for forgetting about the keys, but as tears gathered in the corner of her eyes, mortification set in.

"Hey," Tanner said gently. "It's okay. You had no reason to be thinking about things like that before now. Get dressed and bring your pistol. But I have to warn you, it's going to be a long, uncomfortable night, especially if he doesn't show. We can't risk light of any form, not even a cell phone."

"So it's just you and me, two guns and a toolshed?" She smiled. "You sure do know how to show a woman a good time."

"It *will* be a good time if I can catch him. Then you don't have to worry about keys again."

"That would be nice," Josie said, and she meant every word. But by the same token, she knew that as soon as the intruder was caught, Tanner would leave, and she didn't want him to. She frowned as that realization crossed her mind.

"What's wrong?" he asked.

"Nothing," she replied, quickly erasing her frown. "Just thinking." She wasn't about to tell him what she'd been thinking. She was already confused about what had happened between them earlier and even more worried about how far it might have gone if Emmett hadn't interrupted them.

The worst part was, she knew she wouldn't have

been the one to put on the brakes. As much trouble as she had had in the past with men, and no matter that she'd sworn completely off relationships and was facing eviction from her childhood home if she didn't get her life together, the truth was, she was drawn to Tanner LeDoux in a way she'd never been drawn to a man before.

He challenged her, infuriated her and at the same time, made her feel beautiful, interesting and important. With her ex, she'd thought she was loved, but even in the three years they were together, she'd never felt he was invested in her as much as she felt Tanner was after only a matter of days.

It's his job to be invested.

The thought ripped through her mind, crushing her lofty thoughts. She knew it was true—protecting her was part of Tanner's job—but part of her wanted to believe that he felt more for her than he would for just any employer. Certainly, she hoped he didn't go around kissing all his clients.

"I'll go change," she said, and headed upstairs, hoping activity would break up her thoughts. Not that she had any hope it would last when she was about to sit in a dark shed for who knew how many hours with a man who hadn't uttered five sentences all evening. She and her thoughts were likely to be chilly, uncomfortable, edgy and bored, all at the same time.

She changed from yoga pants to jeans and pulled a hooded sweatshirt out of the closet to wear over her T-shirt when the night air got too chilly for the thin tee. Forgoing her usual work boots, she selected tennis shoes instead, figuring if she had to run, they might be a better option.

As she pulled on the shoes, it occurred to her that if

the creature appeared, they might have to track it into the swamp. She pulled her work boots out, figuring she'd bring them with her, just in case.

When she walked back into the kitchen, Tanner looked over at her and raised his eyebrows.

"You're bringing a change of shoes to the stakeout?"

"I put on tennis shoes thinking they were better for running. Then I thought we might have to go into the swamp, so I brought the boots, just in case."

"I see." He grinned. "And you thought your attacker or a swamp creature would wait for you to change shoes so we'd have a fair shot at him?"

She laughed. "When you put it that way, it does sound silly, but I swear, it made sense in my closet."

"I'm sure it did."

"So, what do you think—the tennis shoes or the boots?"

The grin vanished, and she could tell he was mentally processing all the possible scenarios.

"I don't know," he said finally. "If you don't mind risking a sprained ankle in the swamp, I'd say go with the tennis shoes, especially if it's a significant speed difference. I don't want anyone catching up with you again."

"I think the sprained ankle is worth the risk," she agreed, and placed her boots next to the back door. "Should we bring food or drinks? I've never done a stakeout, so I'm not sure."

"Maybe a couple of bottles of water, but not a lot. There's no bathroom breaks on stakeouts, so it's not wise to drink a lot."

"Right." She grabbed two small bottled waters from the refrigerator. "What else?"

"I've got flashlights and a spotlight. If you've got your gun, then that's it."

She took a breath and blew it out. "Then I guess I'm ready."

He nodded. "Wait here. I'm going to turn off the kitchen lights, except for the light over the stove, then run upstairs and turn on the lamps in our bedrooms. I want him to think we've gone to bed."

Josie nodded as he turned on the stove light and flipped off the kitchen lights. The stove light cast a dim glow around the kitchen, and she stood there in the shadows, peering out into the swamp. Was it out there? Was it watching the lights in the house, just waiting to strike?

Despite the warm temperature in the kitchen, she shivered a bit and turned from the window. No use spooking herself before she'd even left the house.

Tanner appeared a minute later and pointed to the utility room off the kitchen. "The exit off the utility room offers the best cover. There's no light on the side of the house and it's only ten feet or so to the hedges. We can skirt the outside of the hedges almost all the way to the toolshed. Unless someone's using night-vision goggles or can see in the dark, we ought to be able to get to the shed undetected."

"Okay."

"Follow me, and lock the door behind us. I borrowed a set of keys from your spares."

Josie nodded and followed him through the laundry room to the side exit. He peeked out the tiny laundry room window, then eased open the side door and slipped out into the night. Josie turned the lock and followed him outside, gently pulling the door shut behind her.

The night air was humid for December and seemed

to cling to her as she followed Tanner down the row of hedges that stretched down the side of the house to the back lawn. The sound of the night creatures filled the air—insects, birds, frogs and a host of others. It was oddly comforting to her. It felt right, as though everything was in balance.

They edged along the hedges and then paused at the end of the row. Josie peered around him across the vast back lawn, but the dim glow of moonlight offered only a limited view. The seconds crept by, turning into what had to be a minute, and she wondered what he saw that she didn't.

Suddenly, the little moonlight that had been present faded away.

"Now," Tanner whispered, and hurried across the ten-yard gap between the hedges and the shed.

Josie hurried behind him and glanced up before she entered the shed, just in time to see the dark cloud that was covering the moon slip past, exposing the yellow glow again in the night sky.

He'd been waiting for the cloud cover. Smart.

The shed was only six feet by ten feet and with all the equipment it held, only a narrow strip down the center was left bare. Despite the two windows, it was pitch-black inside after Josie closed the door. Her eyes were struggling to adjust when Tanner turned on a penlight.

As he directed the tiny light to the left of her, she realized why no light had entered. During his patrol around the house earlier that day, Tanner had covered the windows with a tarp.

"I rearranged the boxes on each side," he said, "so that they were sturdy enough to sit on. You take the side that faces the house. It will be easier to pick up any movement near the house from the backyard floodlights. I'll take the side facing the swamp."

"Okay," Josie said, and crawled atop the boxes to sit next to the window.

Tanner took the position across from her. "Grab the tarp, but don't remove it until I turn off the light."

She placed her hand on the edge of the tarp, which was looped over a nail, and waited. A second later, he clicked off the light and she pulled the tarp from the nails. With both the windows exposed, the moonlight crept into the shed, casting a dim glow across its path. Josie realized that Tanner had set the boxes up so that they were out of the path of the moonlight as it streamed through the glass.

"Smart setup," she said. He hadn't missed a trick.

"I just incorporated some hunting principles."

She frowned, then mentally chided herself, happy that Tanner couldn't see her face in the darkness. They were hunting someone—or something—whether she liked to think of it that way or not. And if last night was any indication, he was also hunting them.

"How was your visit with your brothers?"

"Fine. Max ate so many of your cookies, he's probably sick. They were really good."

"There's worse things to die from, I guess." She was pleased that her cookies had been a hit but disappointed that Tanner wasn't going to shed any light on their meeting.

It's probably family business.

She sighed. With everything going on in her life at the moment, the last thing she needed was to be focusing on other people's business. If what they'd discussed involved her at all, Tanner would have told her. They'd already agreed to no more secrets between them.

Because men have been so honest with you before.

She tried to clamp down on the thought before it took flight and continued to nag her the rest of the night, but it was too late. A mental parade of every man who'd ever lied to her ran through her mind, so-called high school friends, coworkers, agents, clients, lovers…even her own father, who'd hidden the loss of their money until just before his death and even then hadn't admitted the extent of it.

"I see something." Tanner's voice yanked her out of her tally of disappointment, and she stiffened.

"Where?"

"At the north side of the estate at the edge of the swamp."

"Can you tell what it is?" A lot of creatures dwelled in the swamp and it wasn't unheard of for them to venture onto the cleared grounds.

"No. It's sticking to the shadows but appears to be moving this way."

She licked her dry lips and swallowed, trying to get rid of the lump in her throat. "What do we do?"

"We wait until I can identify it or until it moves to an area where I can leave the shed and try to sneak up behind it."

"Right." She reached down beside her and felt the pistol that she'd laid on the crate next to her leg. She tried to think of something—anything—to occupy the time, but her mind was completely devoid of distractions. All she could think about was the thing moving toward them. Was it her attacker? Was it human? What did it want from her?

Every second that passed felt like an eternity, and she began to count her heartbeats as they pounded in her chest. She wanted so badly to ask him for an update but held back, not wanting him to know how much the situation was getting to her. If she couldn't handle sitting still in the dark, Tanner would never let her go tracking with him, and that's exactly what she intended to do the next day if they couldn't settle things tonight.

Tanner left his seat and inched open the door to the shed, peering outside.

"There," he said, his voice excited. "I see it again, at the edge of the swamp across from the barn."

My horses!

"Is it moving toward the barn?" The fear she'd felt was pushed aside in an instant by the thought of something harming her horses.

"I can't tell. The barn casts a long shadow on that side. If I climb out this window, I won't be in sight. I'll work my way down the hedges and to the backside of the barn. Then maybe I can sneak around to the far side and catch him."

"That sounds good."

"I suppose it's pointless to ask you to stay here?"

"You know it is."

"Then stick right behind me," he said. "If anything happens, run and call the police. Do not attempt to help me."

A rush of bad outcomes started up in her mind, but she pushed them aside, determined to remain focused and calm. As calm as she could manage, anyway. He pushed open the window and slipped outside, then reached back to help her climb out. Once she had two feet on the ground, he released her and hurried down the side of the shed and across the short gap to the bushes.

Hurrying behind him, Josie blinked several times, trying to get her eyes to acclimate to the dark shadows the bushes created. She could barely make out the outline of Tanner's body a couple of feet ahead of her and she picked up her pace so that she didn't fall behind. The last thing she wanted was to lose sight of him.

He slunk down the hedges and then slipped across the back lawn to the backside of the barn. At the edge of the barn, he stopped and she stood next to him, heart racing, as he peered around the corner.

He turned back to her, his expression grim, and waved one hand in the air, then pointed to his ear. She frowned, trying to figure out what he was attempting to tell her, when she realized that the night had gone silent. Standing stock-still, she strained to hear the sounds of the night creatures, but only silence met her.

A footstep on dead leaves broke through the silence of the night like a gunshot. It came from the other side of the barn—the side nearest the swamp. Inside the barn, her horses started to stir, rattling their feed buckets and stomping their feet.

A second footstep sounded and the horses began to whinny and snort. She could hear them pawing at the gates in the barn. They knew something was out there. Something that scared them.

Tanner pulled his pistol out of his waistband and motioned to her to do the same. The pistol was cold and heavy in her hands. She felt her heart beating in her throat as Tanner slipped around the corner of the barn, and she moved quietly behind him. At the other end of the barn, he stopped again to listen.

At first, she heard nothing, and then the sound of sniffing broke through the silent night air. Her pulse spiked and she felt blood rush from her head. It was hunting them—smelling the air to determine where they were. Very little breeze stirred, but what did wafted across them and then past the barn to where the creature stood.

They were upwind!

Josie wasn't a tracker and her only hunting had been with her dad in her teen years, but she knew they had to move or their prey would quickly zero in on them.

Tanner tapped her on the arm and held up three fingers, then two, then one, counting down the seconds until they struck. When his last finger closed into a fist, he launched around the corner of the barn, gun leveled.

Josie immediately jumped around the corner after him, holding her pistol with both hands. At that exact moment, a dark cloud covered the moon and pitched them all into darkness. Twenty yards away, leaves crunched and they both yanked their heads around in the direction of the noise.

Two yellow eyes glowed at them in the darkness and the creature began to growl.

"What the hell?" Tanner said. "Stop right there, or I'll shoot!"

The yellow eyes disappeared and a high-pitched howl rang through the silence, piercing her ears so badly she flinched. A second later, the sound of pounding footsteps filled the air.

"He's running!" Tanner yelled, then took off in the direction of the footsteps.

Josie hesitated only a second before setting off behind him, afraid of what they were chasing, but more afraid to be left behind. What if it circled back around? What if it wasn't alone? A sickening smell wafted past her as they ran and she almost gagged.

The moon began to peek out from behind the clouds as they ran. A dim haze of light inched across the pasture, growing brighter with every step. When the last bit of the cloud slipped away, Josie scanned the edge of the swamp just in time to see a creature with long gray hair slip into the swamp.

She grabbed Tanner's arm and pointed. "There!"

"I saw it," Tanner said, and tore across the pasture to the swamp.

Josie ran as hard as possible, trying to keep pace with him, but was unable to. Her thighs burned with the effort, but she barely registered the fact. When they reached the edge of the swamp, Tanner stopped. The swamp was silent again. No footsteps echoed in the mass of trees and brush.

Tanner pulled out his flashlight and shined it on the ground in front of them, then cursed at the mass of dead vines that covered the ground. He pointed the light at the brush around them and found a broken leaf. He leaned over to sniff the leaf and then pointed past the brush.

"He went this way," he said.

Tanner pushed past the broken leaf deeper into the swamp. He followed the tiny signs that Josie would never have found, especially in the pitch-black night and using only a flashlight. The farther they moved into the swamp, the more the smell of the creature dissipated until it finally disappeared altogether.

The sounds of the night creatures returned and Josie knew the creature was long gone.

Suddenly, Tanner came to an abrupt stop and she ran into him.

"Sorry," he said, and sighed. "The trail ends here, apparently."

Josie stepped to the side to see him shining the tiny light on a three-foot-wide dirt trail that cut through the swamp.

"This is the path to Emmett's cabin," she said, immediately recognizing the path she'd traveled thousands of times.

"Really? Then maybe we should pay Emmett a visit, see if he's home this time."

"Definitely," she said, hoping to put his suspicions of Emmett to bed one way or another. "This way."

She stepped in front of him and followed the trail to the left, deeper in the swamp. A thin ray of moonlight streamed through the canopy of trees, seeming to light the pathway

"His cabin is about a half mile from the main house," she said. "He moved into one of the guest rooms after Dad got sick, but as soon as I came home, he was right back out here in the weeds."

"Do you have any idea how much farther it is to his cabin from here?"

"Not far—maybe about fifty yards."

He walked in silence after that, but she knew the wheels were turning in his mind, putting all the pieces into a nice little box. She hoped like hell that Emmett was passed out drunk or not home. Anything that would convince Tanner her dad's oldest friend wasn't her attacker.

She saw the lights from the cabin before she could make out the outline of the roof. Country music carried through the thin walls and down the path to greet them. Emmett's truck was parked right in front of the cabin.

One option gone. Josie could only hope he was drunk.

They walked up to the door and Josie rapped on it. She heard the scuffling of a chair inside and a couple of seconds later, the door flew open and Emmett glared at them.

"What the hell are you two doing roaming the swamp in the middle of the night?" Emmett's voice boomed into the muggy night air.

Chapter Fourteen

Tanner gave the man a quick once-over before replying. He didn't appear winded and his skin wasn't flushed. There was no smell to speak of except for the coffee brewing in the kitchen.

"We were tracking something," Tanner said. "We caught up to it near the barn but lost it in the cloud cover. I tracked it in the swamp until we hit the trail to your cabin."

Emmett narrowed his eyes and waved them inside. "You said 'something.' You don't know what it was?"

"It was the Tainted Keitre," Josie said.

Emmett sighed. "You know I don't put any stock in that." He studied Tanner for a second. "I wouldn't have thought you did, either."

"I deal with the facts," Tanner said. "It was large and close to seven feet tall. It had yellow eyes and a gray coat."

"You sure it wasn't a bear?"

"Unless it was a gray bear sprinting on its back legs, yeah, I'm sure."

Emmett stared at him for a minute, then nodded. "Let me put on my boots, and I'll help you check things out."

Emmett walked into the bedroom and Tanner scanned the cozy living room, kitchen and breakfast area of the cabin. BBs and gun powder sat in bowls on the tiny breakfast table along with empty plastic casings and a reloading press. Finished shotgun shells were in a plastic tub on the other side of the press.

The coffeepot was half-full and still brewing.

Regardless of how innocuous things looked, it was still possible that Vernon had been the one they'd chased. Tanner hadn't been winded by the time they reached the cabin. Vernon appeared to be in good shape for his age, and not carrying extra body fat like most of the older men Tanner had seen around Miel. Vernon might have had time to recover before they arrived.

The foreman emerged from the bedroom a minute later wearing boots and a long-sleeve shirt. He carried a spotlight and a shotgun. He dipped his hand in the plastic container of shells and stuck a handful in his jeans pocket.

"Where do you want to start?" he asked Tanner.

"I figure we should head back to the main house. I don't like leaving the place unattended with everything going on."

Vernon nodded and they exited his cabin. "We'll take my truck. It's quicker."

They all climbed into the cab of Vernon's truck and made the ride to the main house in silence. The tension was only slightly diminished by the apprehension and fear coming off Josie as she perched on the front seat between the two men, her body completely stiff.

Tanner scanned the house and the grounds as they pulled up the drive. Everything seemed normal, but then, everything had seemed normal right before that thing walked out of the swamp. He shook his head as he climbed out of the truck, trying to clear his mind of what he'd seen standing in the pasture. It had to have been a trick of the moonlight.

Yeah, that was it.

"Let's check out the pasture first," Tanner said. "See if there's anything there."

Vernon nodded and Tanner started across the lawn to the pasture, hoping they found something to eliminate possibilities he didn't want to consider. Unfortunately, what they found in the soft soil near the barn removed all thoughts of trickery.

Vernon shined his spotlight directly at the area Tanner had indicated.

"What the hell…" the foreman said, his eyes wide.

Tanner glanced over at Josie, who was staring at the ground and biting her lower lip, then looked back at the print. The four-toed, semihuman-looking print.

"Maybe a bear got caught in a trap," Vernon said. "Yeah, that's it. Caught in a trap and it damaged his foot."

"Did it make his foot several inches longer and a lot thinner?" Tanner asked.

Vernon frowned but didn't argue. Tanner knew the foreman couldn't identify the print any more than he could. He could also tell that he was struggling to align the facts with something rational. Tanner could appreciate that, as he'd been struggling with the same thing ever since he'd seen those yellow eyes glowing at him.

Vernon shined the light away from the print toward the swamp, but most of the pasture was thick with rye grass. The likelihood of finding more prints, especially in the dark, was slim.

Apparently, deciding the same thing, Vernon turned the light from the print toward the barn.

"Was he going for the horses, you think?" Vernon asked.

"I don't know," Tanner said. "But they were spooked, for sure. They knew a predator was nearby."

Tanner studied the ground between the print and the barn as Vernon's spotlight exposed it, inch by inch.

"There!" He grabbed the light from Vernon and pointed it at a lump of something dark on the ground. "What is that?"

They hurried over to the mass and Tanner shined the light on it. Josie took one look and groaned, turning her head away from the bloody mass of flesh.

Vernon reached down and flipped what was left of the carcass around, studying it. "This wasn't killed here. It's a piece of something bigger, maybe sheep or goat."

"It tore up a sheep or goat and dragged pieces to my pasture to eat?" Josie's voice went up about two octaves.

Tanner looked at the edge of the bone sticking out of the meat and back at Vernon, who was looking straight at him, a worried expression on his face. Tanner knew the foreman wasn't going to tell Josie the truth, and Tanner could tell by the look on the other man's face that he didn't want Tanner to say a word, either.

A million good reasons for lying passed through Tanner's mind, all of them completely valid, if not for the promise he'd made to Josie. By not telling her about his past in Miel, he was already lying by omission. He wasn't going to add to his crime by lying about this, even though it was tempting.

"It wasn't torn apart," Tanner said. "That bone was sawed off."

Josie's hands flew up to cover her mouth. "I don't understand. How could that creature get a saw, even know how to use a saw?"

"It didn't," Tanner said. He walked back to the print and directed the light at the grass, trying to determine the creature's path from the swamp. About twenty yards from the print, he found what he'd expected but had hoped he wouldn't find.

Kneeling down, he ran his hands across the dark, sticky liquid that covered the grass and smelled it.

"Blood?" Vernon asked.

Tanner nodded.

Vernon let out a string of curses that Tanner appreciated and agreed with.

Josie looked back and forth between the two men. "I don't understand…."

"It was bait," Tanner said. "Someone left pieces of whatever this was across your pasture to lure something to the barn. Maybe they figured a bear would pick up the scent. Maybe something else. All I know for sure is that this was deliberate."

He looked at Vernon, who studied the ground, an angry expression on his face. Was he angry because someone was threatening Josie or angry because the whole thing had gotten out of hand?

"It's time to get the sheriff out here," Tanner said, "and make him do his job."

IT WAS AN EXHAUSTING TWO hours later when Josie let Sheriff Reynard out the front door and closed it behind him. He'd been mad and looking for a fight when he arrived, but after Emmett and Tanner showed him what they'd found in the pasture, he got serious really fast.

"You think he's going to look into it like he says he will?" Josie asked.

Tanner stared out the front window as the lights on the sheriff's truck faded into the distance. "Maybe," he said, and turned to face her. "Or maybe he already knows what's going on."

"You think… Oh, wow. I guess I still haven't gotten the hang of this suspect-everyone thing."

"I know it's harder since they're all people you grew up with."

Josie felt tears of despair well up in her eyes and she looked down at the rug, struggling to hold them back. She didn't want to look weak in front of this man who was doing so much to protect her and her home. A man she'd grown to respect in such a short time.

"What's wrong?" he asked quietly.

She looked up at him, and one glance at the concern in his expression had her tears spilling over. He moved immediately to her and gathered her in his arms.

"I didn't know it would be so hard," she said, her face buried in his chest. "I'm looking over my shoulder all the time and questioning the actions and words of people I've known my entire life. I know I should have realized it would come down to someone I know, but I guess I never dwelled long enough on that fact to think about how difficult it would be."

"It would have been harder not knowing. Even if the threats stopped, would you be satisfied?"

She thought about his words for a bit. Would it have mattered? If everything had faded away and she opened her bed-and-breakfast without another hitch, would she have pressed to find the culprit? Or would she have thanked her lucky stars that it stopped and hoped it never happened again?

She leaned back so that she could see his face. "I…I think I would have needed to know. I would have eventually gotten around to where you are on my own, and then I would never have been able to look at the people in this town the same way again. I wouldn't be able to talk to someone or even wave at them across the street without wondering 'was it him?'"

Tanner nodded. "Those kind of things fester, like an untended boil. Sometimes it's below the surface and you can ignore it rather well. It may itch occasionally and sometimes even hurt, but unless it bubbles over the surface, you don't have to face it directly. You just have to find a way to live around it, which isn't always the best option."

His voice was so sad when he spoke and his expression was filled with longing, as if he knew from experience about burying things.

Before she could change her mind, she said, "You sound like you're speaking from experience."

He sighed. "I am, but not in the same way you are. My boil has festered since I was a boy, but I never thought there were any answers to be found. Not until today."

"Your brothers' visit—they were here about old issues?"

"The oldest and biggest issue in our lives. Remember I told you our dad died when I was eight?"

She nodded.

"He was murdered. We were skipping school that day and Holt saw the killer outside the house, but the police couldn't find anything and the trail went cold. Until now."

Her hand flew over her mouth. "Your brothers found the man who killed your father?"

"Not yet, but for the first time in over twenty years, there's a lead on the case—a promising one."

"Oh, I don't even know what to say." So many emotions flooded through her as she thought about the three

little boys who'd lost a father, who might get answers
so many years later. Answers they thought would never
come.

"I don't, either," Tanner said. "When Holt said they
were coming to see me, I thought of a million things it
might be about, but that was nowhere on the list."

There was a tiny ray of hope in his eyes as he spoke,
masked with a ton of apprehension, and her heart ached
for the boy who'd never gotten the answers he deserved.
She lifted one hand and placed it gently on his cheek.

"I hope you get the answers you're looking for," she
said.

He looked directly at her, his eyes seeming to stare
right into her soul. His face was only inches from hers,
his arms still wrapped around her. She'd never wanted
anything more than for him to kiss her right now. Her
entire body tingled with anticipation, her lips quivered
with excitement.

As he lowered his lips to hers, she felt her knees get
weak and forced herself to lock them in place.

He kissed her without hesitation, like a man who
knew what he wanted. She melted into the kiss, into his
arms, silently willing him to want more than just this.

Never had she felt so alive, so sure of herself and her
life, as she did right now—in the arms of this incredible
man who wanted her. His lips parted hers and he deepened the kiss, mingling his tongue with hers.

He pulled her closer to him, and she could feel the
hard length of him pressing against her. Refusing to
think about the consequences, she ran her hands down
his back and up under his shirt, her fingers caressing
his rippled back.

His lips left hers and moved to her neck, kissing
a trail from her ear down to her chest, just above her

breasts. She groaned as he tasted the sensitive skin on her chest. A flash of heat rocked her body and suddenly, she felt as though there was entirely too much material between them.

"My bedroom," she managed to say. "I have protection."

He didn't even hesitate before sweeping her into his arms and carrying her upstairs.

He laid her gently on the bed and pulled her shirt over her head. She unfastened her jeans and pushed them over her hips, wiggling out of them as he tugged them off her legs.

"The top drawer of the nightstand," she said, and he pulled a foil package from the drawer.

In the lamplight and clad only in her bra and panties, she thought she'd feel self-conscious, but when Tanner shrugged off his clothes and looked down at her, there was no doubt that he liked everything he saw.

"You're so beautiful," he said as he slid onto the bed beside her. "Do you know how rare it is that someone is as beautiful on the inside as she is on the outside?"

Her breath caught in her throat. She'd never met a man like Tanner. Never even thought such a man existed. And now she wanted nothing more than to become one with him. To complete something that had started the moment he stepped into her home.

He leaned in to kiss her as he pulled her undergarments away. She ran her hands across his lean, muscular body, certain that a more desirable man had never been created. He pressed his naked body against hers and she could feel the hard length of him on her thigh.

"I want you now," she whispered. "We have the rest of the night to take our time."

His eyes widened a bit and he smiled.

"Whatever the lady wants," he said as he moved between her legs.

She cried out in pleasure as he slid into her, then matched his rhythm until they both went over the edge.

JOSIE WAS STARTLED OUT OF a deep sleep by insistent banging on the front door. Tanner had been sleeping beside her, his arm wrapped around her, but he'd popped straight up at the first knock. The alarm clock read 5:00 a.m. They threw on clothes and hurried downstairs, and Josie worried the entire way. A knock on the door at sunrise was rarely a good thing.

The construction crew leader, Ray, stood at her front door, his face pale. The rest of the crew stood around his truck parked about twenty yards away in the driveway.

"What's wrong?" Josie asked.

"It…the Tainted Keitre tried to kill us." Ray's voice wavered as he spoke, and Josie could see his hands shaking.

"Oh, no! What happened?"

He pointed to his truck and the crew members stepped aside so that she could get a good view. The hood was caved in several inches across the width. Tanner stepped past her and walked over to the truck. She hurried behind with Ray.

"What fell on this?" Tanner asked, his voice grim.

"A tree. If I'd been a second faster, it would have fallen on the bed." He waved a hand at his crew. "They could have been killed."

"Did you see anything when the tree fell?" Tanner asked.

"Only a wall of wood and branches coming at me. I threw the truck in reverse and got out of there as fast as possible." He looked at Josie. "I'm so sorry, Ms. Bettencourt, but we can't continue working here. We have families to think about."

Josie's heart fell, but she couldn't blame the crew. No one should have to risk their lives to put up fencing. It was simply too much to ask others to deal with.

"I understand." She placed her hand on the distraught man's arm.

"If there were any other way…" Ray said.

"Please, don't worry about it. I wouldn't have let you continue work after this, anyway."

The relief in his expression was obvious, and Josie felt a surge of empathy with this dedicated, honorable man. "When I get all this fixed," she said, "I'll call you. If you're interested in working here again, that is."

He nodded. "We enjoyed the work and you are a good boss. You see that the crew has good food and water and the proper tools to do the job. We're all unhappy that we can't continue here. We'd gladly come back if the creature leaves."

"I'll pay for your truck repair," Josie said.

"It's not necessary," he said. "I have insurance."

"At least let me pay your deductible," she insisted.

"Thank you," he said, then looked at Tanner. "Good luck, tracker."

Ray said something to Tanner in Creole, shook Tanner's hand then left. The truck engine whined as it turned over, but it seemed to run fine as the man backed up in the drive, his crew in the bed of the pickup, looking back at her with sober expressions.

"What did he say to you?" she asked Tanner.

Tanner stared at the disappearing truck and frowned. "I'm not certain, but I think he blessed me."

"Blessed you?"

"Yeah, a sorta of voodoo spell of protection. I haven't heard the words since I was a kid, so I can't be certain."

Josie looked down the drive as the truck disappeared around a corner into the swamp. A voodoo spell of protection? She didn't believe in the old ways, but for a moment she couldn't help hoping it would work.

MAX SLAMMED HIS CELL phone down on Holt's desk, jumped out of his chair and paced the length of the small office. Knowing his brother better than he knew anyone else, sometimes even his wife, Holt kept silent and waited for him to pace out the anger so that he could speak.

Not that it was necessary. Holt knew who Max had been speaking to, and his reaction could only mean bad news. It could come in several forms, but the result was the same—no answers.

Finally, Max slumped back in the chair and looked over at Holt. "I guess you already figured it's bad news."

"Kinda hard not to."

"Yeah, well, this is the worst of the bad news. Tanner's guy is dead. Stabbed in a prison riot."

Holt frowned. "And the guy who stabbed him?"

"No one was charged. The guards had their suspicions, but with all the fray, no camera caught it and there were no eyewitnesses. And, of course, they never found the weapon."

"But they have someone in mind?"

"Oh, yeah, and you're going to love this—he was paroled two months ago and hasn't checked in with his parole officer in over a month. And you'll never guess what tattoo he had on his biceps."

Holt sighed. "Another dead end."

"Maybe not. I've asked my buddy to check with the

guards and see if anyone else in the prison has that same tattoo. If this is an organized crime unit, it's likely that some of them are doing time or have done time. We may be able to track one of them down."

"It's worth a shot, but I'll be willing to bet that if they get caught, they disappear completely when they get out. When they reappear, it's in a different area and with a new identity. Given what happened to Tanner's guy, I'm guessing if there's any fear they'll talk, it's taken care of in prison."

Max shrugged. "We have to try."

"We won't stop trying. I promise you that."

Chapter Fifteen

Tanner studied the fallen tree with a clenched jaw. Josie stared at the huge truck in dismay, and he knew she was thinking about what could have happened if the truck had passed underneath just a second before.

"It's rotted," she said. "The creature must have pushed it over on them as they passed."

Tanner shook his head and pointed at the base of the tree. "Not unless he had a chain saw handy. The tree was rotten, but the base was cut. There's sawdust everywhere."

Josie sighed. "I guess it doesn't matter at this point. The result is the same. Whether it's a giant, hairy monster or a psycho with a chain saw, the crew would still be in danger."

Tanner could tell by the tone of her voice that she'd given up. The tree was the final straw. "I have some money," he said. "Let me hire some crews from New Orleans to finish this work."

"No. Even if I had unlimited funds, I can't ask anyone else to work here. If something happened to someone on my property, I'd blame myself."

"Then let me make the bank payment since you can't open on time."

"Absolutely not."

"It can be a loan, if that makes you more comfortable."

"I already owe enough people." She sighed and walked over to kiss him lightly on the mouth.

"It's not that I don't appreciate the offer," she said. "I think you're a wonderful man, and if it would make a difference, I swear, I'd take you up on it. It isn't pride that's speaking, it's practicality. Unless I get the bed-and-breakfast open on time, the bank will call the loan, anyway. I'd have to pay off the entire arrears in order to get another extension."

He knew she was right, but it still made him angry. All that money his father had left him and it couldn't make a difference. What the hell good was it, then?

"So you're giving up?" he asked.

"No! I mean, not unless you are."

"Absolutely not." He wrapped his arms around her and pulled her close to him. "I'm more determined than ever to get to the bottom of this. If I work fast enough, maybe…"

He didn't want to say that maybe it wouldn't be too late. Every day of work lost moved Josie closer and closer to losing her home to the bank. He could buy her house outright several times over, but it would take a month or more to convert the hard assets to liquid in order to get that much cash, and he knew Josie would never accept it, even if he called it a loan.

He told himself that she was too proud so there was no use offering, but that wasn't all there was to it. He knew that if it came down to money changing hands, he'd have to tell her who he was and the thought of revealing that withheld information was something he wasn't ready to face, not until they were completely out of options.

How could he make her understand why he'd held out on her? Why he'd pretended he didn't know her or anyone else in town? How could she possibly understand? Last night was the first time she'd ever really seen him, despite his having been around for a year, and he had no words for how last night had made him feel. He was a coward for not telling her, but he could live with that for the moment. All that mattered was solving the mystery and getting Josie back on track.

Maybe she'd never even have to know everything.

"We're going to figure this out," he said, and gave her a squeeze before releasing her.

A tiny bit of hope sparked in her eyes. "So, what's the plan?"

He pointed to an area past the trunk of the fallen tree. "I start tracking here. The other trails have been dead ends, but sooner or later, he's going to make a mistake. This stunt with the tree was a desperate move. It's clear this tree was cut, and monsters don't carry around chain saws."

"You think he's changed tactics? He thinks by scaring the workers off, he'll get me to give up?"

"He may know your money and time are running out. How many people in Miel know how badly off you are?"

"I…I don't know. I mean, no one knows the details, except maybe Emmett. I'm sure Dad told him before he died, and the fact that he's never asked me for his 'share' of the business is rather revealing."

"And does Emmett know that your dad lost your money, as well?"

"He's always intimated that I should have money to burn from my 'fancy French career,' so I don't think so. I get the impression that he thinks I should just write the bank a check and get back to the regular business of rice farming." She frowned. "The way he does it, though, it's almost like he's prodding me to talk about it, not just stating a fact."

"Maybe he's trying to figure out if you have money, or maybe he was trying to get you to admit that you don't have any money so that he could talk you into selling. For someone who claims to be concerned, he sure is missing from his job a lot."

She blew out a breath. Emmett's cabin had been empty when they'd tried to find him that morning after the visit from the crew, and all attempts to raise him by cell phone had gone straight to voice mail. "I don't know what to think any more."

He nodded. "Then let's stop speculating and go find some facts."

He grabbed his backpack from his truck and passed another to her. "It's got rope, water, protein bars, a flare gun and, of course, your pistol."

She took the pack and pulled it across her back. He slung his pack over one shoulder and slid his pistol into his waistband.

"I'm going to work as quickly as possible," he said. "There's a storm brewing and it will wash away the tracks. I know you grew up here, but you've probably stuck mostly to the trails. We'll be walking through dense growth. Be observant of your surroundings—ground, brush and trees above. Some snakes and spiders can be just as deadly as bear or alligator."

Her eyes widened a little, but she only nodded.

"And there's something else. This swamp isn't... normal. If you get the feeling that things are skewed even more out of balance than before, let me know."

Her relief was apparent. "You feel it, too?" she asked, her voice soft.

"I always have."

JOSIE SWIPED AT HER DAMP bangs, wishing she'd worn a hat. Despite Christmas being only weeks away, it was in the seventies. The storm that was brewing had the humidity up to its highest possible level.

Tanner hadn't been exaggerating when he'd said he'd work quickly. She'd had no idea how he managed to pick up the trail so easily, but they'd moved at a steady clip. So steady her calves were starting to cramp and she'd begun daydreaming about the water in her backpack.

Just when she thought she was going to have to ask for a break, Tanner drew up short and muttered something she couldn't understand. She stepped to his side and immediately had some guesses about what he'd said. The embankment dropped off a good ten feet into the swirling water of the bayou. Another lost trail.

She pulled off her backpack and sat down on a huge rock near the edge of the bank. She found her water and it tasted so good going down that for a moment she managed to forget that the entire morning had come up a loss.

Tanner pulled out his water and took a drink, still studying the bayou and the bank on the other side. He looked back at her and gave her a once-over.

"You doing okay? I should have taken a break already. When I start working, I tend to lose all track of time."

"I'm fine. Don't ask me tomorrow, but I'm fine for now."

He smiled. "I sometimes have people say 'how hard can it be walking around in the woods all day?' Next time, I'll have them call you."

"Ha. I could give them an earful. So, what now? We go back home?"

"That's something I want to talk to you about. Come look."

She rose from the rock, the muscles in her legs already stiffening, and looked down the bayou where he pointed.

"I don't see tracks in the mud on the far bank, but if he walked on the cypress roots down to that tree that spans the bayou, he could have crossed there. If you're up for it, I'd like to try and cross and see if we can pick up his trail on the other side."

Her mind was willing, but her body lodged a complaint. Mentally promising herself a long, hot bubble bath, she replied, "Whatever you think. You're the expert here. If you think there's a chance to pick up the path again, I want to do it."

He nodded and looked up at the sky, then at his watch. "We've traveled mostly southeast for about two miles."

"Only two miles? You're going to make me cry. It felt like ten, at least."

"It's the humidity and the thickness of the brush. It can create a mild sense of claustrophobia, which makes it feel like you've been in here much longer than you have. Are we still on your property?"

"I think so. It stretches about twenty miles out from the main house to the north, south and east. All the rice pastures are closer to town, and across the highway from this swamp."

"Really? I had no idea your property went so deep into the swamp. So the south side stretches almost to town?"

"All the way, actually. The property line ends behind

the row of businesses on Main Street, right where Big Bayou meets the channel."

He frowned.

"What's wrong?"

"Did your dad create roads from town back into the swamp so that he could check his property easily?"

"Yes. It's part of Emmett's job to patrol them a couple of times a week."

"And Big Bayou branches off into a million inlets all through the property." He blew out a breath. "That makes it so easy for anyone to access this side of your property directly from town."

"Oh! I hadn't thought of that, but you're right. I guess anyone could take a car or boat into the property and cross to the main house completely unobserved. Assuming they knew the swamp well enough." She blew out a breath. "Which definitely puts it back to someone in Miel."

"I'm afraid so." He pointed across the bank. "Let's see if we can pick up the trail on the other side—follow it until it runs out, assuming we can find it, of course."

"And if it leads nowhere?"

"Then I'll start finding out where everyone in Miel was this morning when that tree fell, starting with your foreman."

Josie picked up her pack and slung it across her back. "Then let's get going."

They worked their way down the edge of the embankment until they reached the place with the log across the bayou. Tanner scaled the cypress roots down to the log and then turned around to spot Josie as she followed him down the slope.

She held her breath as she stepped across the log. She

was an excellent swimmer, but you never knew when an alligator might be hiding in the brush, just waiting to snag an easy supper. Even an Olympic swimmer was no match for an alligator.

As she took the last step off the log and onto the far bank, she blew out a breath of relief. Tanner, who'd taken her hand to steady her as she jumped from the log, smiled at her.

"Good job," he said. "A lot of people would have quit on the other side."

"A lot of people aren't as stubborn as me."

He laughed. "In this case, that's a good thing. Now let's get busy and save your home."

She stepped carefully behind him in the slippery mud as they made their way up the bank and into the foliage.

"Wait here," he said, and paced off about twenty yards to the right, then turned around and walked past her to the right. About ten yards past, he stopped and squatted.

"There's a footprint here," he said.

She walked up to stand beside him as he rose.

"Is it the same as the others?" she asked.

"It's the same boot print and looks to be the same size, but it's a common boot and size. Still, it's the only print I see around here."

"Then let's see where it leads."

He looked at the surrounding area and pointed behind them to an area where the brush was pressed down a bit on the ground. "There."

He began picking his way through the brush, and Josie fell in step behind him. As she walked, she checked up, down and side to side with every step. The process was very slow and deliberate.

She glanced past the tops of the cypress trees every few steps, worried about the dark clouds that were starting to accumulate in the sky above them. It wasn't supposed to rain until nighttime, and she hoped it held off that long.

It seemed as if they'd walked forever when Tanner stopped again and pointed. "I saw a flash, like light reflecting off glass or metal," he whispered.

She nodded and carefully followed him through the brush. He'd slowed his pace to a crawl, trying to eliminate as much sound as possible, which was difficult on the dry terrain. As they got closer to the place he'd indicated, Josie could make out the top of a truck.

She sucked in a breath and tugged on Tanner's shirt. "That's Emmett's truck," she whispered.

He nodded and she knew his mind was already racing with the possibilities.

They crept up to the road where the truck stood, parked and empty. Tanner scanned the area and then stepped out of the brush and over to the truck to look in the bed.

"He's carrying fertilizer and water hoses back here. Any reason he'd have that stuff?"

Josie shook her head. "It's winter. We're not planting anything right now, and the rye grass is already established."

"Then let's track him down and see what he's up to."

He checked the brush on both sides of the road and finally waved a hand down one side. "He's entered the brush in this area in multiple places. The only reason to do that is if you don't want to create a discernible trail."

"But it's the side away from the house," Josie pointed out.

"Yeah, but the care taken to cover his tracks bothers

me. If he was doing a basic inspection of the property, why would he need to hide?"

Josie bit her lower lip. "I don't know, but I guess we should find out."

TANNER FOLLOWED THE foreman's path through the swamp. About twenty yards into the brush, he found the place where all the entry points met, and it was a simple matter to follow the well-worn trail. As a plus, because so much of the trail had worn down to dirt, their progress was almost silent.

The better to sneak up on secret-keeping foremen with.

As they rounded a bend in the path, a smell that Tanner was familiar with wafted by his nostrils and he sighed. A minute later, they stepped into a clearing in the middle of the swamp. Wood-framed containers covered with chicken wire stood in rows in the clearing. Metal barrels at the end of each row of containers caught rainwater and distributed it to the containers using a makeshift navigation system of battery-operated pumps and garden hoses.

Josie sucked in a breath and stepped up to one of the containers, peering at the green plants growing inside. "Is this what I think it is?" she asked.

"Yes, it is." Emmett Vernon stepped out of the swamp, a shotgun in his hands. "I'm sorry you had to find out this way."

Chapter Sixteen

Tanner mentally cursed himself for not pulling out his pistol as soon as he'd caught a whiff of the marijuana plants. He'd been listening for movement as they progressed, but Vernon, with all his years spent in the swamp, was perfectly capable of moving undetected, especially as they'd stepped into his territory. He'd probably been watching them approach through the swamp.

Tanner clenched his hands, trying to gauge his ability to pull his pistol and fire versus Vernon's ability to lift the shotgun and squeeze one off. Finally, he decided that Vernon would probably get one shot off before he did. He could live with that, as long as that shot wasn't at Josie.

The foreman looked over at him, then glanced at Josie, who stared at him, her eyes wide with fear. He lifted his shotgun and released the shells. "Oh, hell, I'm not going to shoot you!"

The tension in Tanner's back and neck swept out like the tide, and Josie slumped down onto a stump.

"Emmett, what is all this?" she asked. "I know I haven't been able to give you a raise, but I never thought you'd do something like this."

"You've got something going with the general store

owner," Tanner said, "and a buyer in New Orleans, maybe."

Vernon looked at him and narrowed his eyes.

"I heard your conversation the other night," Tanner said.

Vernon nodded. "Then I guess I've got some explaining to do. Mind you, I'm not trying to make excuses. I'm just going to tell you what's going on."

Josie's eyes widened and she rose from the stump, her face pale. "You've got cancer."

"What?" Tanner stared back and forth from Vernon to Josie.

Vernon sighed. "I stopped chemo, hoping I could develop this strain of weed to counteract the worst of the nausea. I'm one of those that pretty much feels that way all the time. The chemo makes it worse."

"I knew you'd lost some weight," Josie said, "and you weren't on top of things like always, but I didn't make the connection."

"How did you make it now?" Tanner asked.

"Because Ted's wife has cancer," Josie said, "and she's sick a lot. I read an article on the flight back from France on medical marijuana. When you brought up Emmett's conversation with Ted just now, it all clicked together."

"And your New Orleans connection?" Tanner asked the foreman.

"A scientist working with me to perfect the strain. He'll apply for the proper credentials if I can get it right." He sighed. "Unfortunately, at the moment, what we're doing isn't exactly legal. I understand that you'll need to report it."

Tanner shook his head. "I'm not an employee of the state any longer, and this is private property. My suggestion is that you talk to your scientist and get all this moved to a laboratory somewhere."

Vernon nodded. "I was about to. He called me yesterday with the particulars and I was going to move the plants on my day off. I started worrying about discovery when all the vandalism kicked up a notch. After what you saw, I knew it wasn't a bear. I was afraid if the wrong person found this, the sheriff would be more than happy to toss Josie in jail."

"You'd probably be right on that account," Tanner agreed. "We tracked you from the bayou to the road, and then picked up your trail to this site. It wasn't simple, but I doubt I'm the only person in Miel who could do it."

Vernon narrowed his eyes. "I haven't been to the bayou in weeks. Not since I got this irrigation system in place. I've been driving up and entering from different places off the main road."

The foreman looked a bit sheepish. "It's not the smartest thing to do, leaving my truck right there, but I've gotten too weak to tromp through the swamp that far every day."

"That's not good," Tanner said, and told Vernon about the workers' narrow escape with the cut tree and the tracks that had led them to where Vernon's vehicle was parked.

The foreman's eyes widened. "Are the men all right?"

"The truck got the worst of it," Tanner said, "but they won't return to work until we can assure them the 'creature' is gone. The 'creature' used a chain saw and left boot prints."

Vernon shook his head and frowned. "You think it was him you picked up from the bayou?"

"Maybe. Same boot type and size, but there's no way to know for sure. But if someone cut across like we did, they probably saw your truck. It won't be long before they go poking into whatever you're doing back here."

"Damn it," Vernon said. "I'm sorry, Josie. I never wanted to make any trouble for you. Lord knows, you got enough already."

"Why didn't you tell me?" Josie asked quietly.

"To what end? So you'd feel even worse about not having money? By the way you've been scrimping and saving, I'd already gotten the idea that your father lost your money as well as his own even though you wouldn't admit it when I pressed you. I don't have insurance and I didn't want you selling your home with that idiot Realtor to help me."

"I—" Josie started to talk.

"That's just what you would have done," Vernon interrupted. "I know you, Josie. You're just like your mother, who was a damn sight nicer than your father."

He gave her a small smile. "She would have been proud of the woman you turned out to be."

Josie stepped over to him and threw her arms around him. "Oh, Emmett. You've been part of my life for so long that I don't know what I'd do without you. We'll figure this out. I promise."

Tanner felt his heart ache just a bit at the sight of Josie holding the crotchety old foreman. He'd completely misjudged the man, and he'd never been so happy to be wrong. Vernon had cared so much about Josie, he'd attempted to hide a deadly illness from her, still doing what work he could, despite the fact that he must feel horrible.

She kissed Emmett on his cheek and Tanner saw his jaw twitch as he hid a smile. Josie was an incredible woman with an enormous heart. The people who really knew her were willing to go to great lengths for her, and that said everything to Tanner. She didn't deserve the problems she currently had.

If it was the last thing he ever did, he was going to see that she got the life she deserved.

JOSIE STEPPED INTO THE kitchen and smiled when she saw Tanner making grilled cheese sandwiches. It had been a long, heartrending day, and they were no closer to finding the source of the vandalism than they had been that morning. Her hopes of a New Year's opening were fading so far in the distance that she couldn't even hope they'd be regained.

"How did you know that's my favorite?" she asked as he put the sandwiches on plates.

"Isn't it everyone's favorite?"

She laughed, wondering how it was that he could make her smile, even in the midst of the worst crisis of her life. "You got me there. I'll get the drinks. Soda, wine or beer?"

"Beer is tempting, but I don't want my reaction time dulled. Just water for me."

She pulled two bottled waters from the refrigerator and placed them on the table with the sandwiches before sliding into the chair across from Tanner. "You think he'll be back?"

"Until he gets what he wants."

She sighed. "And we don't even know what that is."

"It all seems to have started when you began construction, so we can only assume they don't want you to succeed in opening the bed-and-breakfast."

"So someone who knows I'm broke."

"And thinks your only option outside of the B-and-B is to sell."

She blew out a breath. "You're back to the selling

again. I know it seems the logical path, but if that's the case, then why hasn't a buyer pursued me more aggressively? Sam contacts me occasionally to ask about it, but I haven't felt pressured in the least. If his client was really serious, wouldn't they be upping the ante?"

"Maybe they want to get the property at a steal or maybe they don't want to draw attention to themselves by offering a higher price. The fewer options you have, the less money you have to take for the property."

"Seems they'd get the best price if the bank forecloses and sells it at auction."

"Perhaps, but it could take a year before the bank put the property on the auction block. There's a lot of foreclosures right now for banks to get processed."

"Okay," Josie conceded. "That makes sense, but we still don't know why anyone would want this property badly enough to harass me over it."

Tanner frowned. "Do you know who the potential buyer is?"

"I've never asked. It didn't seem relevant."

"Maybe you should."

She took a bite of the sandwich and thought while she chewed. The more Tanner talked, the more it made sense, and the more she wanted an answer to that question. Unable to relax until she knew, she jumped up from the table and grabbed the phone off the kitchen counter.

"Sam," she said when he answered. "This is Josie. Listen, I was just wondering about that offer on my property. I'm not ready to make up my mind or anything, but I wanted to know about the buyer—you know, what they intend to use the property for. I wouldn't want to make a decision that's bad for Miel."

"No, no, of course not," Sam said. "I'm not supposed

to give out this information, but as a resident, I share your concerns. The man's name is Frederick Shore. He's a businessman from New Orleans and is looking for a big old house in a small town as a sort of retreat. He'd seen yours in some old article on historic homes and found it 'charming.'"

"Frederick Shore?"

"Yeah. Are you reconsidering? Because if so, I can definitely counter with a better price. I think he'd pay it."

"No, I'm still not ready to sell, but I thought it was smart business to make sure I had a clear understanding of all my options."

"Of course. You know, if you're not busy some night, I could go over the offer with you, maybe over dinner?"

She rolled her eyes at Tanner, who shook his head as she turned Sam down once again.

"I have to give him points for persistence," Tanner said after she'd hung up the phone.

"Yeah, well, he's really racking them up. The buyer's name is Frederick Shore. Sam said he wants some weekend-retreat sort of thing to get away from his business in New Orleans. He saw the house in a magazine and decided he had to have it. It was featured in *Southern Historical Homes* magazine a couple of years ago, so that seems a reasonable story."

Tanner scrunched his brow. "I've heard that name before. Let me call Max and see what he can come up with."

Josie nodded as Tanner called his brother. He gave Max the name and what he wanted and disconnected. The entire exchange took less than a minute.

"That's it?" Josie asked.

"What do you mean?"

"You call your brother and give him a name, and he just gets information for you, no questions asked?"

Tanner gave her a blank stare. "He's a detective. That's what they do."

Josie laughed. "Men are so different. A woman would have wanted to know why you needed the information, had the guy been harassing you and then she'd want to help you kick his butt."

"Women are complicated." He frowned. "Would she really want to kick his butt?"

"If he was harassing me, yeah. That's what girlfriends are for."

"Maybe I need to get some girlfriends, then. They sound handy."

She grinned. "I don't know…multiple girlfriends often present problems for men."

"That's okay. I've always been the one-woman sort."

He looked directly at her and she felt a flush run over her.

His cell phone rang and he glanced down at the display. "Guess I'll stick with brothers for the butt-kicking, then," he said as he answered.

He listened for a couple of minutes and Josie tried to wait patiently until he wrapped up the call.

"So?" she asked, the second he hung up.

"Shore owns a manufacturing plant in New Orleans, so the money part checks out. He's loaded. No police record but plenty of lawsuits from ex-employees, competitors—the usual sort of thing for a big business owner."

"Oh." She couldn't help feeling a little disappointed.

Tanner smiled. "Did you expect a bio that said 'psycho killer who likes to wear costumes and stalk young women'?"

"No, but I was hoping… I don't know."

"I'm new to this investigating business, but my guess is that most criminals don't stand out on paper or in a crowd. Not if they're any good at it."

"They're careful. Yeah, I get that. Although some of the things that've happened here don't seem all that careful. I mean, why let my horses loose? It got me outside, but there was no follow-up. Someone could have taken a shot at me and ended it all right there."

"Some of it seems less calculated, but maybe it's all just aggravation intended to pile up and make you break. A murder would bring down a horde of cops and likely lock the place down until the investigation was over." He sighed. "But I don't know, really. I can't think like a disturbed person."

She crossed her arms over her chest, a chill running over her, even though the kitchen was warm. "Is that what you think—that the person is disturbed?"

"Love and greed can make you do crazy things, but it takes a certain kind of mind to hack up an animal to bait a bigger animal to your barn."

"Yeah."

She stared out the window and into the backyard. The sun had set hours ago and only the back porch lights and the light at the barn entrance pierced the black night. The storm that had been threatening to drop all day was still holding off, but Josie knew that before the night was over, the downpour would come.

Would he strike again that night? She'd locked the barn up tight with a padlock. No one was getting in there without bolt cutters or a blowtorch, but she still worried. As she lifted her sandwich off the plate, she saw something move out of the corner of her eye. Immediately, she dropped the sandwich and jumped up from her chair.

"What is it?" Tanner asked as he joined her standing at the back window.

"I saw something moving in the shadows around the barn."

He grabbed his pistol from the kitchen counter and tossed her the phone. "Call Emmett and stay put."

Before she could protest, he ran down the hallway into the laundry room and slipped outside. Josie punched in Emmett's number and was thrilled when he answered on the first ring.

"There's something moving outside around the barn," she said. "Tanner's gone to check it out."

"I'll be right there. Get your gun and don't leave the house."

The sound of the phone slamming down echoed through her ears. She looked out the back window and realized how vulnerable she was standing in front of all that glass. Her pulse racing, she grabbed her gun and turned off the kitchen light. The laundry room door had a window that offered a decent view of the barn. She'd go there to watch.

And pray.

TANNER SLIPPED DOWN THE hedges toward the barn, listening for the periodic sounds of movement he'd caught as soon as he'd stepped out of the laundry room. Something was definitely out there, and he didn't think it was an animal. The sounds were too vague, as if an attempt was being made to minimize or mask them.

At the end of the hedges, he stood partially hidden in the bush and peered through. At first, he saw nothing. Then the clouds moved and a dim glow of moonlight filled the pasture. At the edge of the barn, he saw someone wearing a ball cap and swinging something large and square in his hand.

A second later, the smell of gas wafted by.

A flash of anger went through him and he launched out of the hedges and set off toward the vandal at a dead run. The vandal froze when he heard the footsteps and glanced wildly around, trying to locate the source. That was all the time Tanner needed to close the gap and tackle him to the ground just as he was turning to flee.

They slammed onto the hard dirt ground surrounding the barn and rolled around in a frenzy of thrashing arms and hands. Tanner managed to flip the guy over and scramble on top of his back, holding his arm up high on his back to prevent him from attempting to move any more.

A spotlight hit him and a second later, Emmett ran up. He pulled off his belt and handed it to Tanner to secure the guy's arm. While he was tightening the belt, he heard the door to the laundry room slam shut and Josie joined them a couple of seconds later.

"You caught him!" Josie said.

"Yeah," Tanner said. "Now let's see who's been causing all this trouble."

He stood and flipped the man over and yanked away the ball cap that had slid down and was covering his face.

Then they all stared in shock.

Chapter Seventeen

"Marquette?" Josie looked down at the angry young woman, unable to formulate an educated question.

"Why are you harassing Josie?" Tanner asked.

Marquette struggled to sit up, then glared at all of them. "Josie, Josie—everything's always about Josie. Prom queen Josie. All the men want Josie. My brother went into the military because you left. Sam hasn't asked me for a date again since you've been back, and now you have him shacking up with you." She pointed at Tanner.

Josie stared at Marquette, completely floored and starting to get angry. "I never dated your brother, I have turned Sam down every time he's asked me out and I am *not* shacking up with Tanner. He is a professional working here."

"Yeah, just like before, but you never paid attention to him then," Marquette spat out. "You never paid attention to anyone but your little crew of rich, spoiled, popular friends."

Josie looked over at Tanner, assuming that Marquette had confused him with someone from their high school days, but one look at his stricken face and she knew Marquette was right. All of a sudden, it hit her—the young boy who worked the fields for her father, the shy kid who sat in the back of the class, the boy with the drunken mother who everyone in town whispered about.

She sucked in a breath, then turned and ran for the house. It had all been a lie. Tanner had never cared about her or saving her home. He was just living out some high school fantasy, and she'd played right into his hands.

Slamming the door behind her, she went to the kitchen and poured herself a shot of scotch. Her hands shook as she swallowed the warm liquid. It burned her throat on the way down and she put the shot glass in the sink, disgusted with Tanner, Marquette, Emmett, her father and even her mother, for dying too young. But mostly, disgusted with herself, for letting down her guard when she'd promised herself she would never do it again.

She grabbed the phone from the counter and dialed the sheriff's department. As soon as possible, she wanted crazy Marquette and lying Tanner off her property. Tomorrow, she was going to call Sam and tell him to get her the best offer he could for the house. She'd give Emmett whatever he needed, then use the rest to get as far away from Miel as she could.

A knock sounded at the front door and she walked to open it while the phone started ringing at the sheriff's department. She yanked open the door, not even stopping to think that it was long past a decent hour to be visiting.

Marquette's brother, Rob, stood in her doorway. A single glance at his face and the pistol he had leveled at her, and Josie knew she'd just made the worst mistake of her life.

JOSIE'S SCREAM MADE Tanner's blood run cold. It took only a second for him to realize that he'd made a critical error in assuming Marquette had been working alone. There was no way she could be the creature. She didn't have the build for it.

"Watch her!" he yelled at Vernon as he took off in a dead run toward the house.

The scream was far too loud to have come from inside the house, so he started at the back. There was no sign of a struggle and the back door and laundry room door were both locked tight. He raced around to the front of the house, and his heart dropped when he saw the door standing wide-open.

Panicked, he pulled out his pocket flashlight and scanned the ground in front of the porch, trying to determine a direction. At the far end of the porch, he finally found footprints in the loose dirt. They pointed directly into the swamp.

He raced to the edge of the swamp and quickly located the signs of passage. Josie was not going willingly. There were no more screams, which meant he'd probably taped her mouth, but the signs of a struggle were detailed like a storybook in the broken branches and vines stripped of leaves. She was doing everything possible to create a trail.

He ran through the swamp, following the signs Josie had left, certain that he'd catch up to them soon. Fear and regret coursed through every inch of his body, and he only hoped he wouldn't be too late to save her. To tell her he was sorry for hurting her. To help her save the one thing she had left.

A thick hedge of brush rose in front of him and he burst through it, then slid to a stop in a clearing. The moonlight streamed down in between the cypress trees, creating a spotlight effect in the small opening.

Marquette's brother, Rob, stood at the opposite edge of the clearing, his arm wrapped around Josie's neck, a gun pressed to her head. Duct tape covered her mouth, and a trickle of blood ran down her forehead onto her cheek. The stark terror in her eyes made Tanner's heart drop.

He'd failed.

"Drop your weapon," Rob said.

"Why?" Tanner asked. "You're going to kill her, anyway, aren't you? Why didn't you just do it at the house?"

"Let's just say I wanted my ten minutes alone with Josie. Ten minutes to torture her like she did me in high school. I thought I'd get to my truck before you caught up with us."

Tanner clenched his jaw, knowing exactly what Rob had planned for Josie's last ten minutes on earth. "The jig is up. We've got your sister."

"That stupid bitch. I tried to stop her, but she snuck out of the house. I figured she was headed here. I told her to stay out of this and let me do my job, but she couldn't resist the chance to get back at Josie."

"Josie never did anything to any of you."

"That's where you're wrong. She was a stuck-up bitch who thought we were all beneath her. When I got the offer for this gig, I couldn't believe my luck. All that money and the opportunity to settle the score with Miel's princess. If she would have just given up and left weeks ago, it wouldn't have come to this. It's really all her fault, you see?"

The glow of the moonlight provided Tanner a clear view of Rob's face as he spoke. What he saw made his heart beat faster. Tanner had no medical training at all, but he'd bet everything he owned that Rob was mad. Completely and utterly insane.

Josie's muffled cries filled the air, and Rob ripped the tape from her mouth with a single pull, then wrapped his arm back around her neck. She cried out as the tape tore her skin and Tanner clenched his hands, wishing for any opportunity to take Rob down.

Then his heart stopped when he caught a glimpse of Rob's biceps as he repositioned his arm. He had the eye tattoo.

"You got something to say?" Rob said to Josie. "Now's the last chance you get. Give me a good reason for your daddy to run around bragging about how you were better than all of us. He was a righteous bag of hot air, that old man."

Her face was wet with tears and blood and Tanner could see drops of blood already forming on her cheeks where the tape had been ripped away. She was scared, but for the first time, he saw something else in her eyes. She was angry.

"I turned you all down because I knew I'd always planned to leave here after high school. You all knew that. If you have a problem with my wanting more out of life than being barefoot and pregnant, then I don't care."

Rob smirked. "And look at what good all those big plans did you. You landed right back in Miel, anyway, but with no money *and* no man. You shoulda taken up with a good man when you had the chance, Josie, and then maybe you wouldn't be losing your family home."

"You wouldn't know what constitutes a good man," she said. "Your sister told me you were married and had a daughter. What's going to happen to them now?"

"They're all going to be fine. Once I take care of you and lover boy, it's all going to be better than ever."

"Who hired you?" Tanner asked.

"A very important man who needs this land."

"Frederick Shore?"

"I see that idiot Sam ran his mouth. Between being a loudmouth and a pansy, that was enough for Shore to know he wouldn't be a good ally for the more delicate work involved in his plan. But that fool Sam will likely get a nice commission off my work once Vernon sells."

"Vernon has your sister. When she gets done talking, he won't sell."

Rob laughed. "You think I told my crazy sister about any of this? She thinks I'm settling some high school score, and my employer has the perfect alibi in place for me. The word of an insane person won't hold up against the word of a multimillionaire, and trust me, Marquette is off her rocker. With Josie gone, there'll be no reason for Vernon to stick around. He'll sell."

Tanner's mind raced, trying to come up with the least-risky option. He wasn't about to stand there and wait for Rob to kill them both, and that's exactly what would happen. Rob had been smart. No one would believe the clearly disturbed Marquette if Rob had an alibi that had been bought and paid for.

He looked at Josie, wishing he could communicate with her somehow. She looked him straight in the eye and gave him a barely imperceptible nod. He felt a surge of adrenaline course through his body. She was letting him know it was okay to take a risk. That she knew they were out of options.

If only there were some way to distract Rob, even for only a second, it might be enough time to get off that one shot that could save them both. Then he realized the swamp had gone completely silent. The thought had no sooner entered his mind that a bloodcurdling howl rang out, piercing his ears with its volume and pitch.

"What the hell?" Rob jumped at the noise and glanced wildly around.

The instant the pistol slipped from against Josie's head, Tanner lifted his gun and fired.

He couldn't risk hitting Josie, so the shot was off to the side and grazed Rob's shoulder. Tanner cursed his aim, but Josie took every advantage and scrambled away from him and into the brush. Tanner squeezed off another shot as Rob leaped into the dark swamp behind her.

As Tanner ran after them, dark clouds swept back over the moon, pitching them in darkness. He saw a glimpse of movement to the right and spun around, slipping in the loose dirt. He regained his balance, but before he could take aim and fire, a blur of gray flashed in front of him.

He heard Rob scream—a terrifying wail that made his blood run cold, but it was too dark to see what was happening. Without any regard for safety, he ran toward the scream and slid to a stop in front of a body that was sprawled on the ground. He pulled out his penlight and shined it on the ground, praying it wasn't Josie.

Relief flooded through him when he saw it was Rob, his chest slashed across his shoulder and down to his hip. Blood poured from the wound, and Tanner knew there was no chance of saving the man. He'd bleed out before they could get him out of the swamp.

As he dropped beside the injured man, Josie ran up beside him.

"It was the creature," she said, her voice shaking. "I turned when Rob screamed and saw it."

"Where is it?"

"It ran the opposite direction into the swamp."

"You're sure?"

She nodded. "Listen."

He stopped talking and realized what she meant. All the normal sounds of the swamp had returned.

"Is he dead?" she asked, looking at Rob.

"Not yet, but he will be soon." As Rob leaned over the dying man, he opened his eyes.

"Why does Shore want this property? Why is it so important?" Tanner asked.

Rob shook his head.

"You're dying. At least give your wife and children some reason to think you weren't as bad as this looks."

He coughed and blood trickled out of the side of his mouth. "He's making weapons in his factory in New Orleans, but there's been some heat there recently and his buyers are afraid the cops will catch on. They want to move the weapons manufacturing somewhere remote…."

"And this property offers a lot of bayous that lead to the shipping channel," Tanner finished.

Rob nodded.

"Not to mention lazy law enforcement," Josie added. "They could have manufactured tanks here and Bobby wouldn't have noticed."

Rob coughed again and Tanner could hear the rattling in his chest. He didn't have much longer.

"The tattoo," Tanner said, "what does it mean?"

"No. They'll kill my family."

"Not if you give me enough to dismantle them. It's organized crime, right? And you guys are recruited out of the military as mercenaries for hire?"

Rob reached up one shaky hand and grabbed Tanner's shirt. "I have a sick daughter. Promise me that she'll get medical care. She's the reason I did this. Promise me, and I'll tell you what I know."

"I promise," Tanner said.

"There's a man in New Orleans who runs it all, but I don't know his name. Shore was only one of his chiefs."

"A man with this tattoo murdered my father, Walt Conroy, over twenty years ago. Why?"

"I don't know. We only know our own assignments."

"Guess, then. Why would these men want him dead?"

"Because he was involved with them and wanted out, or he caught them using his business or money for their interests, and he had to be eliminated."

Tanner nodded. With his father's portfolio of companies and deep pockets, either could fit. It would be up to him and his brothers to find out which it was.

"Remember," Rob said. "Remember your promise."

Rob's head fell back onto the ground, his vacant, dead eyes staring up into the darkness. In the distance, Tanner heard sirens approaching.

"Vernon must have managed to rouse the sheriff," Tanner said.

"I completely forgot—I was calling the sheriff when I answered the door. I dropped the phone, but I bet they traced the call."

"You, Vernon, I don't care as long as someone with handcuffs shows up. We need to get back to the house and let Vernon know you're okay."

He started to walk away, but Josie grabbed his arm.

"Wait," she said. "I didn't get the chance to thank you for saving my life."

"Seems it was the least I could do, especially after the way I hurt you."

"I'm going to give you the benefit of the doubt there,

and assume you weren't trying to hurt me. But I'd be lying if I said I understood why you didn't tell me that we shared a past, no matter how slim."

He stared down at the ground for a moment. Was it really worth it, laying it all out? The chance of rejection was huge, but even worse was the fear of living the rest of his life without taking the chance.

"Since we've gotten to know each other," he said. "I've told you about some of my past. There's a lot more that I've never told anyone, and I don't know that I ever will. This town doesn't hold good memories for me— my entire childhood doesn't. There are some things you're better off leaving in the past."

Her expression softened and he knew she got it. In her own way, she'd been trying to do the same thing by returning home.

"I worked for your father in the fields," he said, before he could change his mind.

She nodded.

"One day, he caught me watching you ride in the round pen when I was on break. He quickly let me know that you were better than me and off-limits. I understand now, why he did it. He loved you and he knew I wouldn't be good for you. But it was a hard thing for a boy to hear."

"I'm sorry my dad said that. It was wrong of him, regardless of his intention. I'm beginning to wonder how much of the animosity against me in this town was created by my focus on leaving and my dad's putting me up on a pedestal."

"Maybe it all played a part, but none of this is your fault. You need to believe that. Greed and envy were the only reasons for this. Mostly greed."

"Well, you're not greedy or envious, so why didn't you tell me the truth?"

Tanner sighed. "If I'd shown up at your door and told you I was the son of the town drunk and had been in love with you since high school, would you have let me in the door?"

Her eyes widened and her mouth dropped open. "In love…"

"I left here as soon as I could, and I had no intention of ever returning. I thought it was the worst karmic joke of the century when my first case brought me not only to Miel but back to the one woman I'd never gotten over, no matter how far I ran."

"But you didn't even know me…. How could…" She shook her head. "You were just attracted to me. That's all it was."

"At first, of course it was. You were a beautiful girl and you're the most gorgeous woman I've ever seen. But it was far more than that. You were smart and worked hard in school. You were kind to people, even when your friends weren't. I heard you chiding some of them one day in the gym for being mean to another student. You huffed out of there and for an entire week, you ate lunch with the guy they'd been picking on and ignored them."

Her mouth dropped open. "I haven't thought about that since high school."

"I have. And every other thing you did that made you stand out from the crowd." He lifted a finger to stroke her cheek. "There is no other woman like you. There never has been."

A single tear rolled down her face and she swiped it away with the back of her hand. "Oh, Tanner, what am I going to do with you?"

"Whatever you'd like."

She hesitated for a moment, and he felt his heart drop. Then she flung her arms around him and kissed him soundly.

"Promise me," she said, breaking off the kiss, "that you'll never lie to me again, even by omission."

His throat tightened. She knew exactly who he was and accepted him, anyway. It was everything he'd wanted and the one thing he'd never expected. The past no longer mattered—yesterday or ten years ago. All that mattered was the future.

"I promise," he said, and lowered his lips to hers.

Chapter Eighteen

"We have to make it fast," Tanner said as they rushed into the general store. "Everyone will be here in an hour."

"I know. I know," Josie said, and jumped out of the truck with a package wrapped in pretty red paper and a gold bow.

They hurried inside and Ted broke into a huge smile when he saw them approaching the counter. He yelled into the storeroom and his wife, Annie, stepped outside to greet them.

"Merry Christmas!" Josie said, and handed them the gift.

"A gift for us?" Annie asked.

"I think you'll really like it," she said.

"Go ahead," Ted said, and watched as his wife pulled the paper off the silver picture frame. Inside the frame was a document.

Ted leaned over his wife's shoulder and started reading. Her hands shook as she read out loud. Before she could even finish, Ted pulled the frame from her hands, placed it on the counter and grabbed his wife in his arms, twirling her around.

Josie and Tanner laughed as he set his wife down and ran around the counter to hug both of them.

"This is the best news ever," Ted said. He picked up the frame and stared at the piece of paper that verified Annie's admission to a drug trial, an almost reverent expression on his face. "I can't believe it's really happening."

"The scientist is thrilled," Josie said. "The clearance came a week ago for his trials. Part of his contract with the drug company was the stipulation that Annie and Emmett were the first in his test group. You're not only going to get the best care in the country, you're going to get paid to do it."

Tears streamed down Annie's face as she came around the counter to hug Tanner and Josie. "It's the best Christmas present ever. I'm going to hang this next to my bed, where it's the first thing I see every morning. Thank you both so much, and thank Emmett for us the next time you see him."

"How's he liking retirement?" Ted asked.

"He's taken to it remarkably well," Josie said. "He's working part-time running a bayou tour business in New Orleans and having a blast."

"Is the Honey Island Swamp monster part of his tour stories?"

Tanner smiled. He and Josie had never completely agreed about what had killed Rob that night in the swamp. They'd found the gray-haired costume in Marquette's apartment, along with a bottle of a rank-smelling musk and an MP3 player with an earth-shattering howl loaded on it. They knew Rob had been responsible for impersonating the beast.

But there were still the unexplained things, like the height of the creature Tanner had chased in the woods that first day, the creature at the barn that had been eating raw meat and the hush that came over the swamp immediately before the creature appeared. Had it been a trick of light and shadows? Had their imagination and the stress of the situation caused them to see things that weren't really there?

They'd never know the answer for certain. What Tanner *was* certain of was that no one had seen the creature since that night, and the swamps remained alive with the sounds of all things living there. Ray and his crew had returned to work, and the crew leader had pronounced the swamp balanced once more.

Tanner's mind turned back to the conversation in the general store as Josie was wrapping it up and telling them goodbye. He shook Ted's hand, gave Annie another hug and they made their way out of the store, almost running into Sheriff Reynard when they stepped onto the sidewalk.

"Merry Christmas," the sheriff said.

His attitude had changed remarkably since the night he'd come out into the swamp to arrest Marquette and call the coroner for Rob, but there was still that last thread of standoffishness when it came to Josie.

Right now, however, not a bit of it showed. He looked at Josie, then down at the sidewalk for a couple of seconds. Josie glanced over at Tanner, who shrugged. He had no idea what was up with the man.

Finally, Bobby looked back up at Josie, a slight flush on his face. "I want to apologize for treating you so poorly. I thought things about you that weren't true, mostly because of high school."

"You don't have to—"

Bobby held up a hand to cut her off. "Yes, I do. I've been holding a grudge against you for over a decade and I want to explain. I asked you for a date in high school, and you turned me down. That was humiliating, of course, as it is for most teenage boys, but that's not why I was angry. There was a note in my locker that evening signed from you. It said that you would never go out with a fat, stupid, poor loser like me and not to embarrass you by asking again."

Josie's eyes widened. "I never—"

"I know you didn't. Marquette left a diary, and I've been going through it with the federal police. She's the one who did it. She was jealous of you way back then. I guess she's what doctors would call unstable. Your return to Miel set her off again, especially when Sam dropped her cold and started chasing after you."

"Oh, wow."

"I'm not the only person she did it to. As soon as I have clearance, I'm going to turn a copy of the diary over to you, and I'm going to contact every person mentioned in there who Marquette waylaid and let them know the truth. We also found a key to your house in her apartment, so I'm sure it was her or Rob who was in your house that night. No telling what they had planned."

"The whole thing is so sad," Josie said. "I know she tried to hurt me, but I can't help feeling sorry for her. It must be hell to be trapped in her mind."

"It is sad, but at least she's got a medical excuse for her behavior. I don't. I understand if you never forgive me, but I couldn't live with myself if I didn't tell you what I'd found and apologize for being the biggest jackass this side of the Mississippi River."

Josie leaned over to kiss his cheek. "Apology accepted. I have a new take on life—no looking back."

"I like that," the sheriff said, breaking into a slow smile.

He looked over at Tanner. "How's the investigation into your father's murder going?"

"Good. It's a massive undertaking that will likely take years to get to the bottom of, if that's even possible, but the New Orleans police and the FBI are dismantling the organization one piece at a time, starting with Frederick Shore."

"Did you ever figure out…" The sheriff trailed off, probably not certain how to word his question.

"Our father's involvement?" Tanner nodded. "We hired a forensic accountant to go through all his company's records from the date of his murder to five years before. His CFO was laundering money through his businesses. They arrested him doing the same thing with a company in Baton Rouge six months ago. When questioned, he admitted that our father was killed because he caught the discrepancies, but claims he had nothing to do with the actual murder."

The sheriff shook his head. "I'm sorry that happened at all, but I'm glad that at least you and your brothers were able to find out your father wasn't involved."

"Me, too."

The sheriff extended his hand to Tanner. "Merry Christmas!"

Tanner shook his hand and gave the man a nod before grabbing Josie's hand and pulling her toward the truck. "Let's get out of here before anyone else sees you and wants to confess their sins."

She laughed and swatted at him with her free hand before jumping in the truck. "They said they'd be here at one. We still have thirty minutes to get everything ready."

"Uh-huh," Tanner said, knowing Josie would think of a hundred other things to make everything "just perfect" before his brothers and their wives showed up for the Christmas Eve celebration.

It had taken some convincing, and Tanner had finally shown Josie a portfolio statement that spelled out just how much money his dad had left him, before she'd accepted money to get the bank off her back. He'd found an unexpected ally in Josie's friend Adele, and had taken an instant liking to the spry older woman. They'd driven her to the airport in New Orleans the day before to catch a flight to spend Christmas with her son, who was stationed in Germany.

Despite his and Adele's pushing, Josie had insisted on going through with the bed-and-breakfast plan because she wanted to make the income for the ongoing payments herself, but Tanner figured sooner or later, she'd come around to his desire of wanting the house all to themselves.

He was a patient man. It had taken over a decade before Josie Bettencourt was part of his life, and he'd never in a million years thought it could happen. Waiting a while longer for complete solitude was a small price to pay.

She'd hired a new foreman for the rice farming—a young man from Miel, who was excited about the opportunity and the salary, and most especially, the cut of the profit that he'd take for doing a good job. With Josie running the B-and-B and training her horses and the foreman handling the fields, Tanner could get back to work with his brothers, helping people who were out of options.

He'd spent a lot of time in the past couple of weeks talking to his brothers. Talking about serious matters— their childhood, their relationships with their father, their mothers and each other. Tanner had been surprised to hear Holt and Max freely admit the issues they'd struggled with because of the past. All this time, he'd thought he was the only one who'd felt damaged, but now he knew his brothers understood his struggles and were happy to talk any time he needed to.

Josie had been a whirlwind at the house, running from room to room and issuing orders for him to move, carry and place. He knew all the effort wasn't necessary, but he had to admit that Josie had her mother's touch. The house had been transformed into a winter wonderland, with garland wrapped around the spindles of the stairwell complete with giant bows spaced evenly upward and poinsettias sitting on each corner of the living room fireplace set off by a huge wreath hanging above the mantel. An enormous Christmas tree, stuffed to the hilt with decorations, stood beside the fireplace, towering up to the second-floor landing.

It was beautiful, and classy, just like its owner, and Tanner felt like the luckiest man in the world.

Josie was carrying a tray of sugar cookies to the living room when the doorbell rang. Tanner could hear his family laughing and talking outside as he waited for Josie to hurry up beside him before he opened the door.

They rushed inside, all shouting Christmas greetings, their arms full of packages. Tanner and Josie helped them unload the packages around the tree. Then everyone exchanged hugs and kisses. Tanner looked over at Josie, who'd wanted this holiday to be perfect, and was happy to finally see her relax as Alex and Colette exclaimed over the house and the beautiful decorations.

Tanner smiled as Josie took them upstairs for a tour of the rooms. His brothers and their wives were warm, wonderful people. He'd never doubted for a second that they'd take to Josie right away. She fit with them, as if she'd been perfectly made for the slot.

And maybe it was that simple. She was perfectly made for him.

Hours later, when they were stuffed with the wonderful dinner and entirely too many sweets, they moved back into the living room to open the gifts. Josie passed a tray of coffee around to everyone, and Tanner waited impatiently for her to set the tray down.

He cleared his throat to get everyone's attention, and when all eyes were on him, he smiled at them. "I'd just like to say that I couldn't be happier to be here with all of you. I spent so many years alone because that's what I thought I wanted, but I was only hiding from my past. What I've come to realize is that I don't have to do that anymore, and I want to thank each of you for the role you've played in making my life as good as it is today."

"About time I get some credit!" Holt yelled, and raised his coffee mug.

Everyone laughed and Alex, Colette and Josie teared up a bit and sniffed.

"And if you'll indulge me one more minute," Tanner said, and reached inside his pocket for the ring he'd bought in New Orleans the week before.

"Josie," he said, "I know it's a lot to ask you to take on, but if you're up for the job, I've got a great family with a hole in it. I don't want anyone in that slot but you. Will you marry me?"

Josie stared down at the ring, then looked back at him, tears in her eyes. "Yes," she said, then threw her arms around him.

"Yes, to all of you."

* * * * *

Special Offers

Every month we put together collections and longer reads written by your favourite authors.

Here are some of next month's highlights— and don't miss our fabulous discount online!

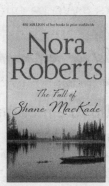

On sale 19th April   On sale 3rd May   On sale 3rd May

Save 20% on all Special Releases

The World of Mills & Boon®

There's a Mills & Boon® series that's perfect for you. We publish ten series and, with new titles every month, you never have to wait long for your favourite to come along.

Blaze®
Scorching hot, sexy reads
4 new stories every month

By Request
Relive the romance with the best of the best
9 new stories every month

Cherish™
Romance to melt the heart every time
12 new stories every month

Desire™
Passionate and dramatic love stories
8 new stories every month